TWO GUN PUBLISHING

Lowell,

Enjoy and stay healthy Marine-

[signature]

11-21

LIAR

TRAIN ROBBER CHRONICLE

WARREN DUNLAP

For information, please contact twogunpublishing@outlook.com

In association with Two Gun Publishing.

9798499322703

To Gary and Clara Gillum

My friends through the tough and tame times of life.

ACKNOWLEDGEMENTS

There are many people who have assisted me in researching information which has allowed me to be as period accurate as possible. I greatly appreciate each one who has provided me with their expertise on their respective areas.

I first want to thank Dr. Jillian Wenburg who has guided my language and usage of it into this book. The professionalism of correct punctuation, grammar, and sentence structure is accredited to her, along with paragraph spacing, etc. I am obliged and grateful to her for all of her efforts and time she has put into reading and editing this book.

The following is a list of people who have provided me with additional information to make this accurate as to the period.

1. Mrs. Janice Robinson, Assistant Director, Audrain County Historical Society, Mexico, MO.

2. Mrs. Jane Monson, President, Dundy County Historical Society, Benkleman, NE.

3. Mrs. Sharleen Wurm, Director, Decatur County Museum, Oberlin, KS.

4. Ms. Haley Aquirre, Archival Records Clerk, Sioux City Public Museum, Sioux City, IA.

INTRODUCTION

Have you ever wondered about those outlaws who got away with the "loot," never to be heard from again?

I have often thought about that and, at various times, began researching these crimes, only to run down a dead end.

I had been reading up on various outlaws in an attempt to write a historical fiction. All the trails seemed faint, only ghosts or hypotheses were left. In pursuing this topic, I was researching bandits of the Black Hills when the names Joel Collins and Sam Bass came under my sights. This, in turn, led me to the first Union Pacific Railroad train robbery. I continued my research, coming across the name of M. F. Leach. Mr. Leech did an interview with a reporter from the *New York Times* newspaper; the interview was printed in the paper on February 21, 1895. When I read the interview, I initially thought that Mr. Leech was spinning a tale. Even the reporter wrote, "Mr. Leech has a propensity to stretch the truth." This, in turn, ignited me to find the truth.

I read newspaper accounts of the day and later magazine articles, none of which corroborated Mr. Leech's story. I continued to dig deeper and came across a book written the same year as the robbery, 1877.

When I finished reading this book, I realized Mr. Leech was indeed telling the truth about the robbery. But, his account of the killing of Jim Berry did have some embellishments. As for the robbery, there was an abundance of detail, including the actual dates and days of the week, along with names of some passengers and the train and station individuals.

In Mr. Al Sorenson's book, *Sam Bass Hands Up! The History of a Crime*, I found he was very detailed in the account of the robbery and escape, but his report of Jim Berry left me a little confused. I reached out to the Historical Society in Mexico, Missouri, and, with their help, was able to put a clearer picture of that event together.

I have attempted to be as accurate as possible describing modes of transportation and how long it might take to travel certain distances. I researched trains, steamboats, stagecoaches, and military forts which were being used at the time of the robbery.

I do hope your interest will be peaked in some fashion when you read my story.

PROLOGUE

It was just past mid October 1944, SayDee Hawg was just finishing her shift at St. Vincent's Hospital. The Superintendent of nurses, Mrs. Wilke, approached her, "SayDee, I know your shift is almost over and you're scheduled to have a few days off. But I need your help. You see there is this elderly man on third floor who they brought in this afternoon. He may not make it until morning. He didn't want us "poking him" with needles but asked for Laudanum. Heavens, that drug has been illegal for over thirty years. We gave him a morphine pill, but he still is restless and has been asking for someone to stay with him tonight. Maybe he knows he's dying and doesn't want to die alone. He's listed as a "John Doe." I'd get one of the other gals, but they are all married with families. I sure could use your help; the next shift is already shorthanded, so I can't spare any of them. Your only responsibility will be to stay with him. You'll need to give him another pill around midnight, and, if he makes it past seven in the morning, I'll get someone to relieve you. Can I count on you?"

There was a brief pause while SayDee thought about her decision. She sure could use the overtime money for her rent and nursing school bill. It would also help in allowing her to travel to the Children's Home Society[1], where she could visit with people who raised her. "Will I be paid for this time?"

---

[1] Began in 1893 by William & Elizabeth Sherrands, in South Dakota, chssd.org/history

"I sign the timecards, so, yes, you will be paid," Mrs. Wilke said reassuringly.

"OK, I'll baby sit him," SayDee replied.

"Good! Grab something to eat and go up to room 315. But hurry, the nurse who's on duty now will leave in twenty minutes," Mrs. Wilke stated, and then walked back down the hall.

SayDee quickly went to the cafeteria where she ate a light supper and grabbed a coffee to go. Heading up to the third floor, she quietly approached room 315. Standing in the doorway facing into the room was a matronly woman.

"Hello, I'm SayDee, I'll take over." Before she finished her introduction, she could see into the room and saw that the old man was strapped down to the bed. "Why is he restrained?" she queried.

The matronly nurse replied, "He was flopping around like a fish out of water. So, I strapped him down, so he wouldn't hurt himself. He is a feisty old bird. Good luck!" She quickly hurried to the nurses' station down the hall.

SayDee slowly walked into the room sipping her coffee. She walked to the closet to see what manner of dress the man wore, hoping to gain some information about him. She picked up the hanger, which held a dirty shirt and a faded, coffee-stained shiny pair of trousers.

"Git what ya came for?" came a strong raspy voice.

SayDee was a little startled but quickly walked to the man's bedside. "I thought you were asleep."

"Well, I ain't. You got me trussed up like some calf. Why? What kind of place is this?" the man asked.

"We restrained you for your own safety," SayDee said in a confident tone.

"Restrained. H--l, I ain't never been restrained cause of my safety. I come here to die, and some s---of-b---h restrains me. You all must be loco," the old man blurted out.

SayDee replied, "If you stop cussing, I'll take the restraints off."

"Cussin', wait til I get wound up. Then you can hear cussin'," came the response from the old man.

The room went quiet; both stared at each other. SayDee stepped closer to the bed and unlatched the strap across the old man's chest. Next, she undid the strap which was just above his knees. Stepping back, she watched his reactions while sipping on her coffee.

The old man stretched slowly, gently rolling to his side and then returning to his back. He alternated moving his arms across his chest.

"Obliged. Sure could go for some of that coffee."

"If you don't mind, you can finish this. I only had a couple of sips," SayDee offered politely.

"But I do mind. I like my own cup, not your leavings. Take me where I can get some. I don't want to lay in this room no more," the old man demanded.

SayDee thought awhile before replying, "Can you walk?"

"Like a newborn calf," the old man exclaimed.

With a quizzical look SayDee said, "What does that mean?"

"You really are green in the wood," the old man snorted. "It means I'm wobbly when I walk."

"You can hold on to me, and I'll steady you!" SayDee exclaimed.

"Not on your life. I got legs that work, and I plan to still use 'em. But I want my clothes; these night clothes or sheets or whatever, are a mite drafty for my taste," the old man exclaimed as he pulled back the sheets. Swinging his legs over the side of the bed, he sat up. "Missy, we ain't been properly introduced, so you ain't seeing my personals. Turn around after you hand me my clothes along with my boots and hat."

SayDee complied by going to the closet and returning with his shirt and trousers, which she laid next to him on the bed. "Where are your under clothes?"

"H--l, I don't wear hen's skin, maybe flannels when it gets cold," snapped the old man.

The old man seemed pretty limber for his age as he lowered the trousers one leg at a time, allowing his legs to slide into the respective leggings of the trousers. Following in the same manner, he quickly had both legs placed into the trousers; he pulled them up as he slid off the bed, landing with his feet on the floor. He then pulled the trousers up under his hospital gown, zipping and buttoning his trousers once he shed the hospital gown. SayDee noticed scar tissue on the front and back of his right shoulder and chest when he was removing his hospital gown to put on his shirt. The old man struggled with his shirt buttons.

SayDee stepped up to help, commenting, "You seem awfully fit for a man on his death bed."

"Just cause I'm dying don't mean I'm helpless. Must be that little pill the doc gave me. D-mn near good as Laudanum," the old man said with a smile showing his yellowed teeth.

"There you go with that cussing again. You need to behave or I'm not taking you for coffee," SayDee sternly warned.

"Cussing, h--l, I'm expressing, can't talk unless you express," the old man snapped. "I thought I told you to get my boots and hat."

The two looked at each other silently. Finally, SayDee turned towards the closet. Upon returning to the bedside, she politely stated, "Ok, just don't express so much."

The old man shuffled his feet along as SayDee led the way to the elevator and the first floor.

SayDee carried two cups of coffee to the table where the old man was sitting. Placing the cups on the table, she sat in the chair opposite from him. The old man grasped the cup with two shaking hands, raising it to his mouth. With a loud slurp, he sipped his coffee.

"My name is SayDee. What's yours?"

The old man paused while he set his cup down. He slowly looked both ways before speaking.

"Where you from?"

"I grew up in and near Sioux Falls, South Dakota. Why do you ask? You do know where you are at?" was her response.

"No reason, just some people come from other places where I've been, so I might say another name," the old man whispered in his raspy voice.

"You're telling me you use different names, depending on what town you are in?" SayDee stated with wonder in her voice.

"Damnation doesn't everybody?" The old man said matter-of-factly.

"Is that why you seem so restless? You don't want people to know who you are? Are you in trouble?" SayDee inquired.

"What are you the law? You ask as many questions as a star packer? If you think dying is trouble, then yup I'm in trouble."

The old man's sarcastic tone caught SayDee off guard, but she didn't respond and just continued to listen. "No, that's not why I'm restless… well, maybe that's a part of it. There is a lot that I want to expel before I die. Isn't it so with you?"

The odd question puzzled SayDee. "What do you mean expel?"

"You must be a greenhorn in this business. When one dies, you expel your last air. You ain't allowed to even take that. So, I need to expel the load I have been carrying, so I can cross over the divide and not have anything keeping me from getting across. I don't want regrets." Finishing his thoughts, the old man took another slurp of coffee.

SayDee looked into the man's bluish-gray eyes before speaking, "You expel your load, and I'll help you cross over. Tell me… what are your regrets? Let's start from the beginning. My name is SayDee Hawg. Would you tell me your name?"

Chapter 1

My mother was Hattie Polly, she was a saint. We came up the Missouri River in 1866, I think I was five maybe six at the time. We traveled with a man named Boris Dietrick, but he was not my father. My mother never said such a thing. Whenever she met anyone, she introduced herself as: "Hattie Polly and my son," finishing with, "this is Boris Dietrick," as she pointed toward him with an open hand.

We came North to Sioux City, Iowa, cause Boris had a job waiting with Mr. Booge.[2] Mr. Booge had a slaughter business, and Boris was a butcher. They cut meat for the new Railroad[3] coming to Sioux City and the steamboat crews, along with others. We lived in a shanty just west of Hell's Half Acre[4], behind the German hotel. We lived in a tar-papered shack with a dirt floor. Boris left once or twice for a week for some reason. Those were days which were happiest for Ma and me.

In the winter I scrounged for wood to heat the shack and for Ma to cook with. Boris would always wear

---

[2] James Booge established the first pork packing business in Sioux City, Iowa, prior to 1866. Siouxcityhistory.org/ notable people, March 1886

[3] The railroad first arrived in Sioux City on March 9, 1868. Siouxcityhistory.org/transportation, March 1868

[4] Wildest area in Sioux City during the steamboat era; it is a small area between Missouri River, Perry Creek, and Prospect Hill. SC 55 Hell's Half Acre pdg

a big apron stained with blood most of the time. He would strap a belt with a narrow sheath for a long narrow bladed knife around his waist. He always hung the apron and belt on the back side of the door when he would come to the shack. When he traveled, he left the apron and knife hanging on the door. He was a big man and he treated Ma very poorly. He told me never to touch his knife that he used in cutting meat. In our fifth winter in the shack with Boris, I was attempting to cut a larger piece of wood into a smaller size to fit into the stove. I was using Boris's knife to hack on the wood I brung in. Unexpectedly, Boris came into the shack. Seeing that I was using his knife, he immediately grabbed me by the hand I was holding the knife with. He yelled, "I told you not to touch this; now, I'll show you what I use it for!" With his big hand wrapped around three of my fingers, he forced me to make a fist, except for my little finger. Holding my fist below the edge of the table with my little finger pressed onto the table, he drew the knife across the tip of the finger, just above the first joint. I remember a sharp stinging feeling; then, the blood came out from my finger. While Boris was still holding my fist, he yelled, "Shut up, welp, I'll teach you!" He then pressed my bleeding finger against the hot stove. My crying and Ma's screaming were drowned out when I screamed. He let go of my fist, and I slumped to the floor.

That day, I learned what fear was like. I learned never to get Boris angry. From then on, the seed of hate for that son-of-b---h was planted.

I did my best to stay clear of him, but I still felt his back hand across my face many times. Ma always seemed to take the brunt of his anger. He would punch her in the body, so the bruising wouldn't show. He used his open hand on the side and back of her head.

We hardly ever had a visitor while Boris was around. But, when Boris left on one of his trips, a Reverend Haddock[5] would come knocking. He would bring me a stick of candy and I listened as he and Ma talked about God and a man named Jesus. We enjoyed his visits, and this also added to our joy when Boris was away.

It was 1868 when the railroad finally came to town. The whole town was celebrating. The railroad promised jobs and a better life for the people of the city, neither of which Ma and I saw. Boris was busier than ever and things kept quiet at the shack. As business picked up, so also did Boris's social life. He spent more time in the saloons drinking more whiskey. The whiskey caused his temper to flare, which, in turn, caused an increase in our beatings.

The railroad continued to build track toward the south, hoping to cross the Missouri River near Omaha. Currently, the settlers had been crossing it by ferry[6]. Both the steamboats and railroads were trying to satisfy the people's land fever. As time pressed on, steamboat

---

[5] Shot to death in Sioux City, Iowa, August 3, 1886, Siouxcityhistory.org/notable-people/29-reverend-george-haddock.

[6] William D. Brown operated Ferry Service between Council Bluffs, Iowa, and Omaha, Nebraska; his business was called Lone Tree Ferry. Omaha World-Herald May 11, 2018 updated Oct 16, 2019 by David Harding.

traffic slowed while the railroad picked up, both in passengers and freight. In 1872, word came that the railroad crossed the Big Muddy with a rail bridge at Council Bluffs, Iowa.

Ma taught me to cipher and read using the newspaper. By reading the paper, I learned about the local events and some news about the frontier. Ma would tell me about all the important people and about the big rebellion between the states, which had just ended. I never had formal schooling, but I never felt like I lacked anything. When we were together in the shack or out wood gathering, we always had good times. As I grew, I helped with more of the chores, especially the work requiring more strength.

It was the year the railroad bridge crossing the Missouri was built. Boris came back to the shack with more hatred than he previously showed. His normal routine was to come in, take off his apron and knife, and hang them up. Ma always had food ready for him to eat, as it seemed to quiet him down some. I'm not sure what the cause was, maybe because Ma was still cooking the meal, anyway, he went off. He hit Ma on the side of the head with his fist. The fry pan fell to the floor, and Ma fell partially onto the wood pile. He was straddling Ma and hitting her in the face with his fists. It all happened fast. My hate boiled over, I grabbed his knife, and I stuck him in the back. He groaned and straightened his back up. Again, I plunged the knife into his back with all the strength I could muster. He slumped over next to Ma, groaning. I wanted him to be dead and hoped he was dying. I looked down at Ma. There was blood coming out of her nose, mouth, eyes, and ears. I stood there waiting for her to speak.

In a faint soft voice, she spoke, “Give me the knife.”

There was a pause, “Run.”

I placed the knife in Ma’s hand, as the thought about Boris waking up echoed in my mind. I just knew he would kill me. Ma’s words and fear propelled me to run out of the shack.

Chapter 2

At first, I wasn't aware of the direction I was headed. Ma had not allowed me to go toward the river because of the dangers lurking there. Leaving the shanty behind in the darkness, I headed toward Perry Creek. It was there we would gather wood. I stopped and laid on the ground to catch my breath. I thought that at any time Boris would be coming after me. Once I had caught my breath, my ears began hearing voices. I raised my head and looked around. Up and down the creek were campfires. Voices from these camps were filling the air. Most of the fires were on the side of the creek I was lying on. I followed the creek upstream being careful to stay low and out of the light of any campfires.

Having past the last campfire, I sat down to devise a plan. The campfire voices were now replaced with the sounds of crickets and frogs. I knew I needed to get away from Boris as fast and far as possible. The fastest thing I knew was the train, so I decided to take it to Council Bluffs. Once there, I could cross the Missouri River and be out of Boris's reach.

I stood on the bank of Perry Creek peering across to the other side. It was a further distance than I could leap, and I had no idea the water's depth. I backed away from the bank, counting my steps. When I felt I was far enough, I took a deep breath and started to run toward the creek. I had one more step to go when I flung myself into the air, still moving my legs trying to go as far as I could. The slow, dark water swallered both legs, and I hoped it would not take the rest of me. My feet hit the bottom. To my relief, I was in water just above my waist. I hurriedly waded to the other bank and scrambled out of the creek. I laid down to listen if the noise I made going into the water aroused anyone. It was still just the crickets and frogs.

I knew the railroad had crossed the creek closer to town, which required me to walk back towards the town and the Missouri river. The closer I got to the town and tracks, the more campfires I encountered. When I came upon the next camp, I came upon I crept up toward the fire to eyeball what, if any, food was out. While lying in the grass, I searched the area with my eyes, making notes to myself of what was setting about and exactly how close it was to the tent where the occupants were hopefully sleeping. The flaps of the tent were open, and the fire had dwindled to a small flickering flame. Pots were set next to the fire, and I was hoping they held some dregs of food. One item which caught my eye was a blanket placed on a log next to the fire. My wet clothes had begun to cool me down, and that blanket was a thing I needed. Crouching, I slowly stepped closer, with my eyes fixed on the legs of the occupants in the tent. Reaching the fire, I stretched out my hand with my fingers extended to determine if there was anything left in those pots. I slowly dipped my hand into one and then the other, both empty. Still watching the tent, I stepped back a couple of paces to where I could reach the blanket. I picked it up with both hands, and I cautiously turned around and slowly walked back away from the light of the fire. Clutching the blanket to my chest I continued walking towards the tracks.

In the distance was a glow bigger than the campfires I had been seeing, I began walking toward that light. Was this glow coming from the torches of people who were looking for me? I sat down, wrapping the blanket around me, to watch the light. I paused for some time studying the light. I realized the glow was not moving nor were there any voices coming from that direction. I got up and walked slowly towards the direction of the light.

The closer I got, I could see the torches were on poles placed along the edge of a platform. I began moving to the far side of the platform. Slowly, the outline of a black steam engine came into view. I sat and let my eyes take in all that I could see. I realized the engine and train cars were right in front of me. The cars extended back toward the row of torches, which gave light to the platform. Suddenly, I caught the movement of a small yellow glow which was moving. I knelt and watched this glow, which seemed to disappear at time and then reappear. Soon I realized it was the light from a lantern someone was carrying. That someone was on the other side of the train, and I was only able to see it when that someone passed between cars. Finally, that someone came around to my side of the train and continued to walk near the train heading back toward the platform. With the additional light from the platform, I made out the figure of a man who soon disappeared into a small wooden house on the far end of the platform.

I stood up and walked backward into taller grass. I shed my shoes and wet britches. Wrapping the blanket around me, I laid down to sleep. My thoughts went back to the shack and the events of the evening. Maybe I really did kill Boris. I hope somebody comes to help Ma. The warmth of the blanket and tiredness overcame my thoughts with sleep.

I awoke to the sounds of voices and hissing coming from the train engine. The sun was high in the sky; its rays were warming. I got to my hands and knees to peer through the grass. There were people on the platform with others walking to get there from the direction of town. I rolled up the blanket and slung it over my shoulder. After dressing, I, too, walked to join the crowd gathering. Before I reached the platform, the train whistle blew, and the people began to climb into the train cars; I did the same upon reaching the first car behind the engine.

I had never been in a train car before and was excited to see what it looked like. The seats in this car were wooden, with a stove at the far end. Walking toward that end, I discovered an outhouse in the corner. I wanted to see if the next car was any different, so I went out the door and climbed down from the first and up into the second. The second car looked identical to the first. The third car also had the same simple seats and layout. I was just about ready to climb into the fourth car when a voice from a man standing next to me said, "Where's your ticket?"

"Ticket?" I responded with the question.

"Yeah, this is a paying train… not for free loaders!" the man said gruffly.

Before I could say anything or run off, a well-dressed man spoke, "Is there a problem conductor?"

"This ragamuffin plans on free loading. I was just going to kick him off, Mr. Marks[7]," explained the conductor.

"Why, this young boy was to meet me here. I clearly forgot to purchase his fare. Here is $10. I'm sure that will cover his ticket to Council Bluffs," the dapper young man stated.

"Yes, it sure will, Mr. Marks," the conductor agreed, as he reached for a small, colored paper from his vest pocket. "Here is his ticket, Mr. Marks. I was just trying to protect the company from free loaders. You do understand?"

"Yes! Good day, Mr. Conductor," Mr. Marks said, as he guided me with his hand behind my back toward the entrance to the fourth car. This car, I learned, was called a Pullman, it had upholstered seats, carpeting and card table. A large table was in the center with stove and two outhouses. Outside the rear door was a large platform where people could stand. My visual inspection and thoughts were interrupted with Mr. Marks' question. "What is your name?"

I turned to answer. My mind was churning trying to think of a phony name that was close to my real name

---

[7] Benjamin Marks, Civil War Veteran, gambler, and business man, 1846 – 1919. Marks ran a gambling business during the "Hell on Wheels" period of railroad history. Opening his Dollar store in Cheyenne. Wyoming, Wyoming Tales and Trails, topic Building the Union Pacific, page 2.

so I would remember. I guess I paused to long because he asked me again, "What is your name?"

I had struck on the name Tad Poole, so looking at Mr. Marks, I blurted, "Tad Pole."

"That is a unique name," replied Mr. Marks. "My name is Benjamin Marks. You can call me Ben. Where are you from?"

I started to say Sioux City, but my attention went toward a man standing on the platform wearing a star talking to the conductor. Mr. Marks seemed to notice where my attention was diverted too, which prompted him to say, "Are you running away?"

I quickly replied, as I studied escape routes, "Yes. I don't ever want to go back again."

Mr. Marks seemed to make an immediate connection with my statement, "Quick! Slide underneath that couch," he said as he opened the back door to the platform.

Momentarily, the door on the front of the car opened. A deputy walked in, "The conductor said you had a young boy with you. Where is he? I have some questions for him?"

"Well, deputy, he must have seen you coming, because I was just asking him his name while placing my bag down. All I heard was the rear door opening and only got a glimpse of his backside as he was leaving the train," explained Mr. Marks.

"Which way did he run off too?" the deputy asked.

"That is just what I was trying to determine when you walked in," replied Mr. Marks.

With that information, the deputy left the train car.

Mr. Marks sat at the table and told me to stay under the couch until he told me it was safe to come out.

Three other well-dressed gentlemen came in and joined Mr. Marks at the table. I laid under the couch admiring how smooth-talking Mr. Marks seemed with lies. Not a shred of truth did he speak to the law. Why did he shade the law? I thought about that. Was his name really Ben Marks?

Once the train moved away from the platform, Mr. Marks said, "It's alright to come out now." I crawled out and began looking out the window as the scenery seemed to flash by. The men settled into chairs at the table as Mr. Marks took out some paste boards and the four began playing a game of cards. Their attention was focused on the game, and nobody seemed to care why I was there.

My attention was drawn to the outhouses, as I had never seen one in a train, and I was curious. There was some sort of tank up on the ceiling and a chain which, when pulled, would allow water to flow down a pipe into the jonny and empty onto the tracks below. I must have pulled the chain one too many times because someone yelled, "Stop playing with the plumbing!" Going back to the couch, I sat watching the landscape run past. Soon, the warmth of the sun brought on drowsiness. I didn't resist and was soon fast asleep.

I was awakened with the shaking of my shoulder

by Mr. Marks along with his words, “We’re at Council Bluffs, if you want to cross the river, you can stay with me.”

I sat up looking around, thinking the sooner I cross the river the more distance I would be away from Boris.

“What do you say you and me get something to eat? I’m hungry. I didn’t eat anything all day,” Mr. Marks stated as he reached for his bag.

I looked at him and shook my head in approval, all the time wondering how I would pay for the food.

We walked together without saying a word. The café was a short distance from the train platform where we arrived. After opening the door, Mr. Marks went to a table against the back wall. All of this was new to me, and I wasn’t sure what a person was to do so I remained quiet.

“We’ll have two specials, a coffee, and a glass of milk,” Mr. Marks directed his order to the man who approached our table after we sat down. When the man turned towards the kitchen, Mr. Marks continued, “Tad, I think I can use you. Would you like to go to Cheyenne?”

With a big grin, I replied, “I surely would, but I have no money for a ticket.”

“I kind of figured that, so I’m going to hire you to be my watchman. You see, I’m shipping a lot of valuable items to Cheyenne for the store I plan to open. I just want someone to watch over the items to make sure they all arrive in good shape. I think you can do that for me. In turn, you'll be getting a free ride to Cheyenne. Does that sound like something you can do?"

Excitedly, I replied, "I'm sure I can handle watching over your items. When do I start this job?"

"We can cross the river just as soon as we finish eating. I don't think I could take another step without something in my stomach," came the smiling reply from Mr. Marks.

I thought he was a mind reader, for I was about ready to faint from starvation. We ate our meal in quiet. At least I couldn't say anything if he did ask me something; I always had my mouth full. He even ordered me a slice of pie to finish off the meal and a second glass of milk. I felt awfully stuffed after that meal.

While crossing the river, Ben explained that he had to conduct business on the passenger train, and I would be riding with his store items on the freight train whenever it left.

We made our way to the train freight yard where Ben went into a building to talk with the freight man. He came back out with some papers in his hand, and we proceeded down a row of freight cars. Stopping at the second to the last car, he turned as he said, "Here we are. This is the car which will carry my items. Over here on the platform are the boxes which they will load into the car. Each box has a number, and each of the numbers are listed on this sheet of paper. You and I will now make sure each numbered box is shown on this list. You tell me the number, and I will find it on the list and check it off with my pencil. Understand?"

"Sure," I said as I began searching the first box for a number. It was close to dusk when we finished checking the boxes.

Handing me the pencil and papers, Ben said, "I want you to check off each number as they load the boxes in the morning. That way I will know if all the boxes were put in the car. Do it just as we did this evening. I told the freight man that you would be sleeping in the car tonight, and I paid him money for your fare. Will you be alright staying her tonight and riding alone to Cheyenne? It's a long journey."

"I will be fine; I will watch over your items closely and make sure they all get loaded tomorrow," I said, confidently.

With a smiling face he said, "Let's get you some food to take along and get back here before it becomes too dark. I want to be sure you get settled in. Ok?"

After the sun was up, they began loading the freight cars. I watched the workers load the end car and then began loading Mr. Marks's items. I told them I was the watch man and was to make sure all the boxes got into the car. It didn't seem like a big thing to them, but they called out the number on the box as it was brought into the car. All the boxes were loaded, and they shut the door on the items and me. This was before the railroad sealed the cars with 60 penny nails. I could still open the door from the inside. I spread the blanket out and the sack of food along with the jar of water. I was excited to get moving, so, when they began banging the cars together, I just smiled. It must have been some time in the afternoon when the train got going. I opened the door slightly to peer out but wasn't particularly interested in the flat prairie I saw.

Afternoon gave way to dusk and then darkness fell. I stretched out and fell asleep listening to the rhythmic click clack of the wheels against the steel track.

It seemed like I slept all night, but, when I awoke, it was still dark and the train wasn't moving. I slid the door open enough so I could stick my head out. I looked both ways hoping to see or hear something. There wasn't a sound, not even the hiss of steam from the engine. Opening the door, a little further I jumped down to the ground and walked toward the front of the train. I was two cars away from where I started when I stepped off the track bed to pee. With that business finished, I continued my walk towards the engine, but there was no engine. I turned around and walked back to the car I was riding.

Just as I came abreast of the freight car in front of the one I was riding in, a figure appeared at the opposite end of the line of freight cars. I thought I should quickly get to Mr. Marks's car and close the door thus protect his items. A shadowy object emerged out of the darkness in the area between the two cars and struck me in the face. My knees buckled, as I caught the ground.

Chapter 3

"Just wait one minute," SayDee said, "you're telling me as a young boy you stabbed a man and then ran off with a stranger and within a few days someone clubs you and you don't even know where you are at? Mister, you sure can tell a tall tale."

The old man narrowed his eyes and spoke, "Are you calling me a liar? I told you I was going to expel what's on my mind, and I can only do it one time. You can doubt all ya want, but only the end will bear out truth or tale. Now, I'll continue after I get something to eat."

SayDee went back to the cafeteria counter and picked up a roll, which was all that was left. Walking back to the table, she spoke, setting the roll in front of the old man. "I apologize, it was rude of me to interrupt you. This is all I could get, please continue."

The old man reached for the biscuit while speaking, "Just set your fanny down in that chair, so I can carry on." He took a couple of bites, chewed a few seconds, slurped coffee, looked at SayDee then spoke.

"The warmth of the sun awoke me, but I could not see. I rubbed my eyes, which were covered over in dried blood. I stood up and could only stagger around in a circle then fell back down. Feeling my eyes, I could tell they were swollen shut. I laid there with my face to the ground. I must have passed out or fallen asleep 'cause the next time I awoke, it was cooler, and I could see no light through my eyelids. Again, I stood up; this time I wasn't as dizzy. I stood there listening and using my senses of smell and feeling. There was a slight breeze blowing onto me. I walked slowly into it. Every few steps, I would stop and smell and listen. I don't know if I just walked in circles or a straight line, but, soon, I laid down and went back to sleep. The next time I awoke, it was light out. It seemed now I was able to peer out the slits under my eyelids. Everything was very hazy and not in focus. I staggered around, and then I heard hooves pounding the sod. I stood still waiting for the Indians[8] to get me. I had heard there were many Indians in Nebraska. I squatted down hoping not to be noticed and waited for fate.

"Boy, what in blazes are you doing out here?" came a loud clear voice. I stood up and attempted to face the direction the voice came from. I now could hear footsteps pressing down the grass as this person approached. I then felt a strong hand on my shoulder, which turned me around.

"Here, take a drink!" I heard, as a canteen was pressed up to my mouth. I drank deeply of the cool water. I could hear cloth being handled and then water being poured out. A cool cloth was pressed onto my forehead with wiping motions as the man's voice said, "You been here long? This blood is plenty dried. I'm going to put you on my horse, and then I can take you to get more help. Can you talk?"

---

[8] This is the term used during this period of time for all Indians regardless of nation or tribe.

I responded with a weak grunt.

He hoisted me onto his saddle after he tied the cloth around my head. Mounting up behind me, we rode off.

My next recollection was waking up lying next to a wagon, hearing two men talking about me. I still could not open my eyes completely. I was only able to peek out if I tipped my head back.

One of the men asked me my name, but I remained quiet. I hadn't thought of one since I didn't know who these men were. A cup was placed in my hands, and I lifted it to my mouth. This water tasted cool and sweet; I drank it all. Another cool damp cloth was tied around my head, I laid back down and fell asleep.

I was awakened by the sound of men moving around talking as they stood in line at the end of another wagon. The smell of food being cook got me to my feet, as I staggered toward the other wagon. One of the men yelled out, "Hey, the poddy[9] is awake!"

With that announcement, a man in a big apron steered me to the back of the wagon. He poured some brown soup mix into a cup saying, "This here beef stew should help ya. Set here next to this wheel, you'll be out of everybody's way."

He was right; by the time I finished the first cup, I

---

[9] Term used for an orphan calf or to describe a person without living parents.

was feeling some better. He came over with his big ladle and filled the cup again, not saying a word.

Later that morning, a lone rider came into camp. He and the cook talked briefly, and then he walked in my direction.

"Howdy, my name is William Burnham[10] of Austin, Texas. We're bringing a small herd of steers to Kearney. I happened to be riding back from Ogallala when I came across you. What happened to you? Where are your folks?"

I tilted my head back and said, "My name is Tom. I was walking next to a train, and that's all I remember. My folks are dead. Can I stay with you?"

Mr. Burnham put his hands on his hips as he spoke, "We'll have to see about that, in the meantime, you stay with Mr. Books. He's the one wearing the apron. Understood?"

I shook my head up and down.

Mr. Books told me I needed to earn my keep, so he assigned me the job as hoodlum. I was to gather and chop wood, get water, peel potatoes and wash dishes. I

---

[10] Owner of 2700 head driven to Schuyler, Nebraska. Potter, *Nebraska Cowboys of the Open Range*

slept in the cooney[11] of the hoodlum wagon[12]. Thus, I became a member of a trail drive into Kearney, Nebraska. This was, for me, a short drive, only a week, but long enough for me to get a taste of something I thought I could do.

I went to Texas with Mr. Burnham, where I learned to ride and take care of horses. I informed him I wanted to go on the trail again up to Nebraska. He told me it would be the following Spring before any herds would be heading up north. I learned all I could about handling horses, which included how to put shoes on 'em. That Spring, Mr. Burnham did not have a herd going North, I was upset, but he told me I didn't know enough about handling horses let alone cattle. I watched the cowboys work and began breaking horses, I seemed to drift toward the occupation of a bronc fighter, but I never thought myself good at it. I had told Mr. Burnham that my name was Tom Heckrich. Most just called me Heck.

In 1874, Mr. Burnham said I could join the cattle drive heading up the Great Western Trail going north if the trail boss would hire me. He cut me loose and gave me a horse so I could get to San Antonio. I arrived in February and began looking for a man named Mack

---

[11] A canvas tarp fastened to the undercarriage of a wagon used to hold wood or buffalo chips.

[12] The wagon used to carry the outfit's gear, bedrolls, extra water, and cooking equipment.

Stewart[13]. Upon locating him, I explained I had been on a drive before as hoodlum but now I wanted to go back north and was willing to work jingling horses[14]. Mr. Burnham had written a letter of introduction for me and, upon reading what it said, he hired me. The drive was to leave near the end of April, 1875, arriving late July or early August. Ogallala, Nebraska, was the destination for the cattle, and the horses were to be sold to ranchers along the Platte and Loup Rivers, further up North.

There was a total of fourteen cowboys, which included the cook and trail boss. Most of the cowboys were from Texas, although a few were from Missouri. They all knew how to work the cattle and were a proud bunch; they were all rebels and proud of their heritage and occupation. Most were a few years older than I was, with the hoodlum being the youngest, at twelve.

Each one of us had to sign a paper called Article of Agreement, which was the rules of the outfit. If there was a trifle[15] the outfit would determine the punishment, including hanging. Most of them wore guns and were very familiar with their use, having been in the war. We

---

[13] Trail boss of 2500 head of cattle headed north in 1876. *History Nebraska,* Cook's Cattle Drive North 1876.

[14] The term punchers use for the person who brings horses into camp to be used for that day of the cattle drive.

[15] Any argument between punchers on a cattle drive.

made our last stop in Texas at Doan's Crossing[16] to procure the provisions we needed on the drive.

These trail cowboys were made of harder stuff. Everybody knew his duty and nobody shirked it, or they would be ridiculed out of the outfit. No deadheads ever stayed long on the drive.

My job was to make sure the hundred or so head of horses would be brought into camp in the morning for the cowboys to get their mounts for the day. Then, I would move the horses to the next location the trail boss had picked to graze the remuda during the night. I would usually move one or two miles away from the camp.

I came up the trail with the good and the not so good. There was Hi Bernard[17] and Jim Cook[18], who were good cowboys and knew their jobs well. But, the further along one rode, the more you knew what the other cowboys thought, and how good he was at his job. All were whang leather[19] tough.

Those were long, hard days, some cold, a few wet,

[16] The last place in Texas to pick up ammunition and provisions before crossing into Indian Territory along the Great Western Trail.

[17] Manager of Ora Haley's Two Bar cattle ranch in Brown's Hole; he supplied horses to Tom Horn while he was in that area. Wyoming tales and Trails, topic Tom Horn, page 3.

[18] He first came to Nebraska driving cattle in 1876 and settled in Sioux County, Nebraska. *Nebraska.History* , Cook's Cattle Drive North 1876.

[19] A leather razor strap

most hot, and always dirty. Each one of us got $30 a month, except the trail boss. He got more. There were no complaints, at least which were spoken in camp. The cook ran the camp, and you ate what he made and liked it. The closer we got to Ogallala, the slower we moved the herd so as not to burn off too much profit. But the cowboys itched even more to let her rip to h--l and gone.

Ogallala was a day's drive away, as we set around the fire that night. Another trail herd was in front of us, and we had to wait out a day before bringing ours in. One of the boys commented, "Ogallala is the Gomorrah of the cattle trail."[20] Everybody was getting anxious and wanted to cross that river to get into town. Our turn finally came, and the herd crossed first and then the horses. The horses were kept along the river a few miles from town. I stayed with the horses and the chuck wagon for three or four days. Finally, some cowboys showed up with Mack Stewart, and we moved the horses to a large corral. There the herd was divided up, with those cowboys taking a portion of the herd. By the end of the week, only a dozen or so horses were left. Mack Stewart and I drove them to an Indian agency a couple of days to the north. Upon our return to Ogallala, he paid me my wages. I had never had that much money before. I bought myself new boots, some rivet waist overalls, and a saddle. I got a room at Mrs. Gast's Ogallala House, where I got a hot bath and slept in a bed. This was the first bed I remember ever sleeping in. I picked up a

[20] (Adams ##)

paper and remembered how my mother taught me to read from it; there, I read about the discovery of gold in the Black Hills. I thought that might be an easier way to make a dollar than what I was doing, so I planned to head to the Black Hills. Mr. Stewart gave me my best horse, and I felt primed and proud as I trotted towards Sidney, Nebraska, to catch a stage to Deadwood Gulch Dakota Territory.

Chapter 4

"Would you like me to get you a blanket? This cafeteria is a little cold," SayDee asked.

"I'd be obliged, along with another cup of coffee," the old man responded, almost respectfully. SayDee returned with a couple of blankets and two cups, one of water and the other steaming coffee.

In an attempt to show her interest, SayDee spoke, "I'm listening to your expelling and haven't heard anything that a person might be ashamed about."

"I said I was obliged for the coffee and blanket. You could kindly sit and listen," snapped the old man, trying to commence his story.

"It seems to me you are blowing me a windy. You tell of nearly killing a man. Then, someone knocks you out along the rail line only a few days later. I say you are either telling me a tale or you have the worst luck of anybody I ever heard of," SayDee said, half sarcastically.

"In my younger years I might have cuffed you. Now I'm more genteel. Just sit and shut up for a spell," the old man smirkingly stated.

"I rode the stage cause the Indians were still wild, and I felt I would have protection with fellow travelers. When I bought my ticket, I used the name Tom Barnes; I just felt I needed a new name for a new country. I bought a ticket on a Barlow coach; they are not as sturdy and less expensive than a Concord stage. It was a mud coach to boot, which means it had no doors or canvas that could be rolled down should it rain. But near the end of July and August, it ain't the rain you want to keep out, it's the blazing sun and its heat and that constant dust.

There is a portion of that route which requires the team to go up a long sandy hill. The passengers are asked to get out and walk up the hill, thus lightening the load. I said I would ride my horse around the hill and meet them at the top. This agreed with the driver and the messenger. I rode off to make my way up the hill. I hadn't been gone but five minutes when I heard a pistol shot. I reined up and listened. It was the only shot I heard. Maybe, I thought, somebody killed a rattler. I continued my way. I had arrived at a point where I could see the stage stopped part way up the hill and the passengers standing alongside with one mounted masked man holding a rifle on the driver and messenger while the other masked man was taking valuables from the passengers. I pulled my pistol and fired into the air. The outlaw with the rifle fired at me and he hit his target; I tumbled out of the saddle. I must have laid there a while before I regained my wits."

"Why didn't anybody from the stage come to your aid?" SayDee asked.

"I found out later they thought I was one of the outlaws and the rifle shot was just a signal to me. Now, can I go on?" the old man asked, annoyingly.

"My saddle horse stood close by, and I was able to get up on him and rode down to the stage route, but there was no stage around. I followed the road but was getting weak and tired from loss of blood. I guess I blacked out, cause when I awoke, I was leaning on my horse's neck in front of some building. I hollered and then blacked out again.

When I came to my senses the next time, I was lying on a straw mattress in a small room. Next to me on the floor was a pitcher of water and a small basin. My arm was trussed in a sling, and my shoulder was wrapped in some cloths which had blood seeping through. I tried to get up but didn't have the strength. I took some water from the pitcher to quench my thirst. I laid there for a long time listening but heard very little. Finally, sleep overtook me again.

The pain in my shoulder became very sharp; it felt like somebody was poking me from the inside. I wanted to wake up, but my head and body seemed weighted down. Next came a burning sensation with the smell of flesh as at a branding. All my senses seemed to tell me, "This is real," yet my body didn't respond as it should have. Next, came a tingling sensation, first on the front of my shoulder and then on my back, but there was no sensation of being rolled over. Finally, there was a powerful smell of some sort of herbs, none of which was familiar to me. Eventually, I awoke and realized the poultice which was tied under the cloth bandages was producing that god-awful smell. The room was dark with no light shining inside or out. I laid staring into the dark for the longest time until I heard small footsteps approaching. As light as they sounded, I thought it would be a child. Instead, when the door opened, with the backdrop of a sky full of stars, the outline of an

Indian girl appeared in the door frame. Not knowing if she knew I was there, I kept quiet. Only when she kneeled next to the mattress did I realize she knew exactly where I was. First, she felt my head then slowly ran her fingers down my face over my eyes. Stopping just below my eyes she lifted her fingers off my face moving them to feel the bandages next. Before she stood back up, she placed her pointer finger against my lips and gently pressed. Then, standing up, she turned to the open door exiting while closing the door behind her. I listened to the soft footsteps as they distanced themselves from the room. I remained awake for hours. A thin veil of light peeked into the room from around the door frame. I realized she wanted me to remain silent for some unknown reason, and I did so.

She came back after sundown. Her routine was the same, but, this time, she left some bread pieces and added some water to the pitcher. No words were exchanged, and she spent very little time with me. After three days of this, I was beginning to regain a little strength. On the fourth day, she found me sitting up on the mattress. She brought bread and a small piece of jerked meat. She always checked me first, before she would leave any of the food. It was nice to have somebody around, but I was craving to talk with her or anybody. The next day, after she checked me, she pulled on me to stand up. I succeeded, with some effort. After she pressed her pointer finger to my lips, she held up her left hand, palm up, and made a movement with two fingers with her right hand to show a walking movement, then again, pressed her one finger to my lips.

After she left, I realized she wanted me to practice walking but to be quiet about doing it. I practiced often and was stable by the time she returned the next day.

When she returned, I was standing, kinda wobbly on the mattress. She grabbed my hand and led me out of that small room, moving quietly but quickly. Walking a short distance, I recognized my horse tied to rabbit brush. On the trail drive, it was necessary for me to be able to recognize horses in the dark and I definitely knew this horse to be mine. Before she let go of my hand, she placed a beaded object into it. As it was dark, I wasn't sure what it was. She pointed in a direction with her one arm outstretched and brought it out back toward her body; she motioned with her two hands in an up and down fashion without touching; then quickly pointed with outstretched arm in the direction she previously pointed to. I understood her to be saying I needed to leave and ride in the direction she was pointing. I didn't know how to thank her or even what she looked like, but I just smiled then mounted and rode off.

I rode the rest of the night; as daylight came on, I found a place to lay down. I was weak and lightheaded. I laid on the ground face up, and I tied my horse to my side. I was still holding the beaded cloth in my one hand.

I was awakened when somebody began kicking at me. I opened my eyes to see four Indians staring down at me. One held the beaded cloth the Indian woman had given me, and then they motioned me to get on my horse. I did so, and my reins were stripped from my hands by one of the Indians. We rode for a few hours before we came to their camp.

They pulled me off my horse and sat me in the middle of their camp. The women and children gathered around and stared. It was hours later before some Indian leader came to me and spoke in broken English. His name was Blue Horse[21], he was the leader of Wagluhe Band of Sioux[22]. At first, I thought I was going to be a dead man. But, he talked with me, and explained Black Robe; Father DeSmet[23] told the Sioux[24] that if Gold was found in the Black Hills, their land would be taken from them. He also said that he had heard of a three-day battle at Gettysburg in which there were 50,000 casualties. He knew then what the white man meant by a battle. He wanted to know if I was looking for the Gold. I told him I wasn't but was heading north to scout for horse buyers. He told me the Land of Grandmother, meaning Canada, could use horses. He also told me the beaded cloth was from his daughter. She had married a soldier and was not happy, but this beaded cloth is a sign I should go and bring her home. He instructed me to stay at their camp until Spring, then I would be free to go to Grandmother's Land.

Some medicine man came and placed a new

---

[21] Chief of the Wagluhe Band of Oglala Lakota, a warrior, statesman, and educator, 1822 – 1908. *Military.wikia.org/*Chief Blue Horse

[22] Wagluhe is known as the "Loafer Band,", one of 7 bands of Oglala Lakota.

[23] A Flemish Catholic priest, 1871-1973, called friend of Sitting Bull.

[24] Sitting Bull, Lakota Teton Dakota Indian who united the Sioux nations for their survival.

poultice on my shoulder. Each night around the fire, Blue Horse would ask me questions about the white man. After a week or two, I was able to go with them on hunting parties for food. They prepared my food while allowing me to sleep next to the fire at night. I was given a buffalo robe for a blanket. By the end of my stay with them, I had more respect for those helping me, especially for Blue Horse. His wisdom seemed to exceed that of many white men.

When Spring came, a couple of men led me out of camp heading North. We rode the day in silence. Stopping, they pointed toward the direction I should ride. I started off, and I continued trotting for an hour. When I turned to look back, they were nowhere in sight. I still had my money from the trail drive, along with my pistol, horse and saddle. By now, I was ready to get back to some type of city. I laid down and slept until daybreak. In the morning I headed into the sun until I came upon a small settlement, and the people there wondered why I hadn't been killed by Indians. I told them I didn't see any, not wanting to cause trouble for Blue Horse's people. I was just looking for Deadwood in Dakota Territory. They informed me I was in Canadian Territory and needed to head south four days on the trail, which passed their settlement. That night, I struck out toward Deadwood Gulch. Before morning of the fourth night, I arrived at Deadwood Gulch. I had never seen such activity in my life. It was as if the town never slept.

I headed toward the livery stable, my horse and I were tired and hoped the livery man would allow us to bed there until rested. When I saw a blacksmith shop next to the livery, I had an idea.

Upon waking the livery man, I asked if my horse and I could bed down. He told me the charge, and I said I had no money, but I knew how to handle horses and was a good horse farrier. The livery man paused, thinking, then agreed that my horse and I could stay if I shod[25] his horses. I was pleased cause my horse and I found our rest, and I kept my cattle drive wages.

[25] Term used if preparing to shoe horses or after one has put shoes on a horse.

Chapter 5

"My mother lived in Deadwood for a while. Did you ever hear of a woman by the name of Johanna Hawg?" SayDee asked, excitedly.

"Can't say as I have. Upon my arrival, there were no women, at least I never saw one. Women began arriving about a year later and they were the sporting girls."

"My mother worked at the Gem Theater[26], I think she was an actress or something," SayDee interjected, eagerly.

"I know the Gem Theater, what else did your mother tell ya about Deadwood?" the old man asked with curiosity.

In hopes of possibly learning more about her mother, SayDee replied, "I was six and a half when she died, she had made arrangements for me to live at the Children's Home Society. Mother told me she worked at the Gem Theater but only for a while and then went to a place called the Mint[27]. She said it was awful dirty and muddy in Deadwood but most of the area was like that.

---

[26] Owned by Al Swearingen, this establishiment masqueraded as a saloon in Deadwood. It was a notorious brothel. (Bryant and Fifer)

[27] Opened in 1876 by Kitty Leroy, a dancer, gambler, prostitute, and trick shooter. Shot dead December 6, 1877, by her husband, who then shot himself. True west Magazine.com/article/Kitty LeRoy

She also told me how evil the place was, with most people looking out for themselves. The people at the Children's Home told me my mother came from a Hawg ranch and that is why I have my name, from the family ranch where she lived."

The old man studied her for a spell before he spoke. "Was your mother a looker?"

"What do you mean?" SayDee responded with surprise.

"Would you yourself say your mother was a beauty, a good-looking woman?" the old man asked, candidly.

Reflecting on her memory, SayDee paused before answering. "I would say she was pretty, not strikingly beautiful. Why do you ask that kind of question?"

Leaning in closer, the old man looked SayDee directly in the eyes when he answered.

"I don't have time to say this politely and I never thought I'd be in this tight spot. But this is the truth as I know of that time and those places. It was a time of the doer, and to most it didn't matter what you were doing. The Gem Theater was kind of a theater and they did put on some plays but only once in a while. If a woman worked there, she was a saloon gal working to get the patrons to buy drinks or a dance hall gal selling chances for a dance. If she was neither of those she would work in the parlor. Almost all the women that came to the Gem worked in servitude. They owed the owner for their room and board and were obliged to work it off in one of those ways and possibly do some acting. I never saw a play there myself.

The Mint was owned by a woman who had quite a reputation, she was a beauty by anyone's definition. She could shoot straight and throw a knife just as straight. She ran a gambling house and parlor and treated her painted ladies better than the owner of the Gem. Be that as it may, those gals made their money the same way as those at the Gem. As more gold dust came out of the mines, the miners paid the girls with a "pinch". Meaning they would pay with a pinch of dust. A pinch was about twenty dollars. They expected a lot for that price. No need to explain further, I think you know my meaning.

As for the hog ranches, I'll explain it this way. At the top of the pile would be the parlor houses, in the middle would be what was called "bawdy" houses and at the bottom were hog ranches. The hog ranches were located along the stage routes or near forts where the soldiers would have easy access. The women there were a bit tawdry but were just like the rest of us trying to make a go of it.

I know it was hard times then and provisions and what nots cost a lot. These gals had to make it on their own and many were just there to make some money same as those minors and the rest of us. So, a looker always ended up in the parlor houses where everything was more expensive and so those at the Hog ranches were just able to get by. It was a terrible life for them and depending on your status would determine if you could save money to get out of the business or maybe they would try to get someone to marry them. Some became alcoholics or addicted to drugs and some committed suicide because of hopelessness.

I think your mother tried her best to get out and eventually succeeded. You are the proof of her victory.

The two sat there in quiet. SayDee in her thoughts of her mother and the old man in his thoughts of his allurement to those places for his own selfishness. He realized he could have very well-known her mother or at least been in the same saloon or establishment with her. It brought him up short in how selfish he was in those years. Just looking out for his own satisfaction and not being concerned for anyone else plight.

He stared at SayDee to determine if there was any resemblance to him. He slowly stood up and gingerly stepped toward the bathroom.

Chapter 6

The old man was staring out the window into the darkness when SayDee came up and spoke.

"It's time to take one of those pills to help you with the pain. I brought you a glass of water. Do you want to lay down now?"

The old man held out his hand as SayDee put the pill into his palm and then handed him a glass of water. He swallowed the pill and had a couple of sips of water.

"No. Don't believe I would. I'd like to sit outside for a spell," replied the old man without looking at SayDee.

"There is a patio just out the door. Will it be too cold for you?" SayDee asked.

"No. I will take these blankets. We'll be fine. Besides, soon I'll be cold all the time." The two slowly shuffled outside.

"Please continue your expelling of your story," SayDee requested.

The old, man having wrapped himself in the blanket, continued.

"Spring rains of 1876 had set in, and I was relieved to have a roof over my head and a dry place to sleep. My arrangement with the livery man was working out well. I was even able to make extra money by breaking horses. It was my first time I ever worked at a town job. I kept to myself most of the time, and, with the frequent travelers coming in, I always seemed to know what was going on in the area and country. Once in a while, I even was given or found a newspaper from Cheyenne or Omaha.

I saved the extra money I earned from breaking horses. My hope was to buy horses and take them further north and sell them, even selling them to the Indians. While being occupied in such endeavor, I came upon a very bad bronc. He bested me and, in the process, broke my leg. The livery man took me to the doctor's office. He set my leg then gave me a small bottle of Laudanum for the pain. I only took a few drops to get as much relief as I needed. But knew if I kept this bottle and its contents, it may come in handy in the future. I placed the cork in secure and wrapped it with cloths and stashed it away.

I was still trying to gather horses in hopes of breaking them and taking them north. My plans changed after receiving the news about General Custer. I knew if I tried to sell horses to any of the Indians, even to those who befriended me, I would get into trouble. Still the thought of bringing them to Canada appealed to me.

In early October, I started out toward the Canadian border in hopes of getting $20 a head for this remuda. I had gotten about one day's ride away from Deadwood when I met two men on the trail.

There is a saying that meeting one person on the range is a circumstance, while meeting two people it might be a red-letter day. This phrase means it could be good or could be bad situation. This wasn't a good day. They stole my horses and pitched my pistol. I first spent time locating my pistol before following their trail. When darkness fell, I quit the trail and waited until light. At the big river, the Missouri, I lost it completely. I rode back to Deadwood mad about my luck and stupidity. I stewed at being taken advantage of by others. I continued through the next winter working at the livery.

The livery stable and blacksmith shop proved useful in allowing me to find out what was going on in the surrounding areas. Stages were being held up on runs from Cheyenne to Deadwood. At the end of March 1877, a Mr. Collins came to get a shoe put on his horse. He asked me if I liked working this hard for my money. I told him I tried to get ahead with breaking and selling horses but got swindled out of that venture. He asked me if I would like to get my hands on some of the gold being found. Of course, I said I sure would, but I'm not sure working that hard is worth all the results. He asked if I'd be interested in obtaining some gold without all the hard work. "Sure would!" I said. He told me he and his partner, Sam Bass, had the same thing happen to them running a saloon. He thought I should join in with them and make some easy money. Besides, they were shorthanded and needed another man. It sounded good to me, and I left the livery and blacksmithing job.

I joined up but didn't really do much. We attempted some stage robberies, but it was just small pickings. I thought I should have kept at the blacksmithing and bronc busting. We hobnobbed with other outlaws, mostly playing cards and drinking. I wasn't much good at either one. Most of this was done at the Spring Creek stage stop. Our camp was about a half day's ride from that stop. Besides myself, the other five members of the gang were: Sam Bass, Joel Collins, Jack Davis, Bill Heffridge, and Jim Berry. Since they didn't know me well, I said my name was Tom Nixon, although they knew me as Tom Barnes from the blacksmith shop. Bass and Collins seemed to be the ramrods of the gang, and the others were like me: cowboys who came up short on the trail or miners whose luck played out. Either way, we all had no work and were drifters looking to make some easy money. I talked very little and listened more to what they were planning, which came out a couple of weeks later.

They, like me, had been taken in by schemers and were trying to make some good money, then head back to Texas or Missouri where they were from. I told them I was from Canada, and I also wanted to make some good money to purchase a ranch. To me, it seemed like this alliance was of convenience for all the parties. Their plan was to attempt to go after a bigger prize than a stage. They planned to rob a train.

Chapter 7

"Did you lose your senses? Why would you join up with people who were breaking the law?" SayDee stated, emphatically.

"To survive! In those times, some of us did what we thought it took, right or wrong. Just like I was telling you about your Ma. There was no law. Most folks fashioned their own security. Yeah, now, in these civilized times, it sounds terrible, but, back then, it was how we lived," the old man said flatly.

"How could you lower yourself to do that? Didn't you think you could have been shot? Weren't you afraid of being caught and going to prison?" SayDee asked, in an attempt to understand the old man's thinking.

"I didn't think I was lowering myself, more of pulling one's self up to a higher level," the old man said.

"We spread the money around to saloons and gambling houses, along with some of those other places I mentioned earlier. There were outlaws moving all over the place in those parts. We weren't the only gang operating in that area. Besides, I had already been shot," the old man said, justifying his actions.

"How old were you then? Didn't they know you were just a kid?" SayDee asked, curiously.

"A kid?" The old man's voice loudened when he replied. "I was fully grown; I was almost as tall as any man. What a man was to himself is what counted, not how much he knew or how old he was. I didn't act like a kid; I acted like a man. But I did see a kid once in another gang. I guessed him to be a 16 or eighteen-year-old. He was called Charles "the kid" Condon[28]. He sure was out to prove to everyone he was somebody but ended up being nobody. He was a skinny little guy but wasn't afraid to pull his pistol and use it. Now, he had no sense. We all knew it and left him alone."

"Is this your story then? Or is there more to expel?" SayDee asked, expectantly.

"Let's go back inside and have another cup of coffee, and I'll finish it for you," the old man requested.

When SayDee returned with the coffee, she found the old man still wrapped in the blankets sitting at a table near the window. Placing the coffee near him, she asked, "Are you getting tired?"

"Yeah, but I want to finish expelling, and then finish my will if you'll help me," the old man said in a soft voice.

"Sure, you just keep expelling" SayDee said, encouragingly.

After a few swallows of coffee, the old man lifted

[28] Kid Condon was tried Feb. 5, 1879, Federal Case # 35 charged with robbery of U.S. Mail; Feb. 17, District case #30 charged with assault and robbery of George English. Feb. 20, 1879 found guilty, sentenced to life, Wyoming Territorial Prison, escaped on April 7, 1880 recaptured May 18, 1880, April 1, 1885 transferred to Detroit House of Correction. Wyoming State Museum Trial archives. On October 28, 1890, he was given a Presidential pardon on account of his feeble health Indianapolis Journal, 2, October 29, 1890.

his head and began again.

One evening, when the air had just started to turn cold, we struck out for Nebraska Territory. We rode a day, maybe two or three days, until we holed up in a canyon at the very north end of a place called Ash Hollow. Sam went looking for horses. I told him I had a good strong gelding, and I was satisfied riding him. Sam agreed but left with Davis to obtain additional mounts for us. Collins, Heffridge, and Berry rode to Ogallala on some business. I thought that was strange, but I kept my mouth shut. I just stayed out of sight and hung out close to camp. A couple of days had passed before I saw Sam and Davis bringing five horses back. Time passed a little quicker with others around. I examined the horses Sam bought and found them to be very sound. Sam knew how to pick good horse flesh.

Collins, Heffridge and Berry came in two days later. Collins handed out some red neckerchiefs for each of us. These were to be used as our masks for the hold up. Berry strutted around in his brand-new boots, bragging how expensive they were. Heffridge mentioned those boots cost him every penny he had. I paid Berry little mind. He was the oldest, having ridden with Bloody Bill Anderson during the war. He was a real bad man, but I had already figured him out. He drank too much, and he had a dripping mouth. I didn't care much for him at first meeting.

SayDee quickly interjected, "Did he have some sort of medical problem with his mouth?"

"Naw!" the old man was shaking his head as he

spoke. "It means he talked a lot."

Where was I? Oh yeah! That night they talked specifics as to what each one of us was to do. Since none of them had ever done robbed a train before, it was new for all of us. We went over our routine every day for a week or more. Each man had to know his part and know what the other was supposed to do and when. This was done so if one got shot or needed firing cover, we would know where they were. I was to hold captive the station agent and train crew and anyone else they sent to me. Davis went to the engine and was to put out its fire. He would then join Collins, Bass, Berry, and Heffridge at the express car. After the express man was secured, they went through looking for valuables. Finally, they would go through the passenger car and sleeping car to rob the passengers. When it was time to leave the train, we would head for our borrowed horses. We practiced how this would take place every night for over a week. We practiced in the dark, because we planned to board the train in the dark.

It was Tuesday when we struck camp in the late afternoon on the 18th of September, 1877, and we headed south toward Big Springs, Nebraska Territory. We crossed the North Platte shortly after leaving our camp. We rode casually toward our destination; barely a word was spoken except from Berry. We were always on the look-out for anyone else, especially when we rode in the open. Six riders would definitely bring curiosity to anybody's mind.

We first got a glimpse of Big Springs on the edge of the north break of the South Platte River. It was dusk and with a full moon rising; there was enough light to make out the tiny station. It was remote, and that was why it was chosen. There wasn't much there: water tank, depot house, section house, and the agent's house with outhouse. We had to get the agent to hang out the red light to stop the train. Big Springs was not an assigned stop for the Express train. The red light meant they needed to stop to pick up mail. Before that, we had to secure the station agent and especially his telegraph key. Collins seemed to know a lot about telegraphs.

We rode closer to the station until Collins signaled us to dismount. We tied our horses out of sight of the depot house and train. We tied the red neckerchiefs over our faces so not even the station agent would see our faces. Davis and Heffridge each pulled their two guns, and we all walked into the station house. Collins took the telegraph key and threw it outside, while Bass cut the telegraph wire. The station regulator clock showed 10:45p.m., and we had the agent hang the red light. Within a few minutes, the train was pulling to a stop at the water tank. With guns drawn, we all escorted the station agent to the express car, except Davis and I went toward the engine to secure the engineer and fireman. The station agent spoke to the express man, requesting him to open the door. As soon as he did, two of the gang slide it all the way open and Bass climbed into the car and secured the express agent's gun. Two other gang members climbed into the car with him, I took the express agent, station agent, and train crew under guard, allowing Davis to join the others. My gun was shaking in my hand from my excitement. Shortly after moving the captives away from the train, loud whoops came from the express car followed by three wooden boxes hitting the ground. Sam, by accident, found three wooden boxes filled with gold coins. Next, the gang headed toward the passenger car. There were two quick shots fired. That scared me; I thought we were in for a fight. I found out later that Sam shot at a fella that didn't follow his orders. There was a third shot fired, but I think that was just to get folks' attention. I don't know who noticed the west bound freight train approaching first but that ended our pillaging the passengers. The boxes of gold coins were emptied into two seamless flour sacks we brought along. We all moved quickly toward our concealed horses. Our instructions were to head south toward the river, which we did.

"How badly hurt was the person who got shot?" SayDee asked, excitedly.

"Sam said it was a hand flesh wound," replied the old man. "But Bill Heffridge roughed up the express agent pretty bad in an attempt to get that safe[29] open. We were less than a mile away when Sam and Collins slowed and dismounted, distributing some of the gold to each person's saddle bags. At first, only Heffridge and Bass's horses carried all the gold. Now, it was distributed to everyone's horses. We then continued on riding south until we crossed the South Platte."

"You mean you and those other men got away?

[29] This safe was bolted to the floor of the rail car. Only two people had the combination, the one who loaded the safe at the point of origin and the other was the person who was to unload it at the point of destination.

What all did you steal?" SayDee asked with amazement.

"It seems I caught your interest now. But you're getting ahead of me. Just sit and listen. I need to expel all of this as I recall it. It wasn't until much later that I learned what all that train carried[30]," the old man softly stated.

[30] In the through safe was $300,000 in silver bullion; two passengers who were being robbed were successful at each hiding $400. The sleeping car was not robbed because of the oncoming freight engine. The passengers in the sleeper car had $1,000 -$2,000 worth of cash.(Al Sorenson, pp23, 29, 31)

Chapter 8

The old man continued.

I never did think this next part was a smart move by Collins, but he was the one who schemed up this plan. To this day I'm not sure it was smart. Collins wanted all of us to ride into Ogallala and mingle among the town folks and cowboys. The next day we would meet where the gold was buried, and ride south with the cattle herd. I was to stay with the gold all night, since I hadn't been in town with any of them much before. That part I was glad about. We dug a shallow hole and buried the plunder. The cash money was divided up among each of us. We each got just over $460. I was mighty pleased with that sum, but we all knew there was a whole lot more buried in the hole. I was threatened by every one of the others if I confiscated the gold. I told them not to worry; "I'm a good watchman. I'll be here in the morning," I told 'em. Off they rode to Ogallala. I stayed hidden in the brush near where the gold was buried. I checked my pistol to be sure I had all my cartridges loaded. I put all but $60 into the bottom of my boots and the rest into my pockets. I leaned against a stump and eventually fell asleep. The sunlight awoke me, and I began wondering if they got caught. It was about midmorning when Bass and Davis came riding toward the brush where I was hidden. I stayed out of sight. They called out, and I responded. After dismounting, they handed me a new pair of waist overalls.

"What is this for?" I asked.

"Something to put your gold in," Bass said with a smile. Bass and Davis were two Texas boys, and they stayed close to each other. Bass always seemed to be a jovial, carefree individual. I think he really enjoyed the excitement of robbing.

The three of us stayed hidden until around noon when the others came riding out, leading a pack pony and laughing out loud. When we asked what was funny, we learned Collins told the townsfolk they would volunteer to look for the robbers but were unable because they would be herding cattle south this day. We all got a laugh out of it. We dug up the gold and placed some of it on all the horses. We then left the brush riding a few hours south to mingle with the cow herd heading south. We caught up with them just past noon.

Moving cattle is a slow job, and, when you have something that you want to do, like dividing up gold, it really goes slow. The herd had only made about eighteen miles from Ogallala, when the herders decided to bed the herd down for the night. We all took our turns guarding the herd and sleeping with the herders. We did this for two days and nights moving at that slow pace. Beginning the night of the third day, Collins made excuses for all of us to leave the herd. We continued to ride through the night, always heading in a southerly direction. We stopped at the Republican River, where we pitched camp for the night. Our ride through the night was punctuated with laughter and talk of dreams that could be fulfilled. We all conjured up ways to spend our share. We speculated on the amount of gold we had taken. We secured the horses and then bedded down for the night.

Tiredness overcame us; it must have been that the excitement and daring adventure which pumped our blood previously now left us, and the result was bone weariness. We posted no lookout, since we didn't think anybody was following us.

It had been five days since we robbed the train and, having slept well the night before, everyone was ready to eat and get started heading south.

Monday night, the fifth day, we again rode in a southerly direction. By dusk we camped in a thicket near a small creek called Beaver. There was plenty of laughter and jokes. Berry seemed to bring a tone of reality to us when he asked, "Do you think anyone recognized us?"

Collins replied, "If somebody recognized us, we never could have left Ogallala. Remember, I offered to join the posse. H—l, if we would have done that, we might still be there." Everyone laughed. Collins continued, "I don't want to be sneaking around the country afraid of every other man being a star packer. Tomorrow, we'll separate and then head back to Texas in pairs."

Berry, of course, had the last word. He conjured up the idea that he's going to tell his family and friends back home he made a ten-strike in the Black Hills and sold his claim to a Californian for a bag of yellow shiners. I said I would go with him back east to his home. Why I said that, I don't know, since I didn't really like him. Maybe it was because Collins had selected routes to Texas for us to follow. Maybe that's why I said something about going east with Berry, and it would be quicker for me to get back to Canada.

When the counting or sizing was done, we all were more than satisfied with our shares. There was $60,000 in $20 gold double eagles minted 1877. I thought all my dreams and hopes had come true. Deep in my heart, I wished I could get back to see Ma and buy her a house. I never dreamed there was such an amount of money.

Berry piped up again and spoke what we all were thinking, "This sure beats robbing stagecoaches! Collins, you should have thought of this scheme before."

Collins then stood up and explained that if any of us got caught, we were not to give information on the rest. If anyone got in trouble, the rest was to do whatever they could in their power to help them out. He made us swear an oath to this.

About the time we finished this oath, we heard a twig snap. We all froze and put our hands on our pistols. Then we just listened. Davis and Bass got up and walked around the camp to see if anybody was about. When they reported nothing in sight, we concluded that it was the horses. Our talk then drifted to being caught. Collins said if he got in that box, he would not allow himself to be taken alive. We all agreed we would die game[31] wearing our boots. With this, Collins administered another oath which we all swore to.

The rest of that evening we spent sewing up the

---

[31] Die fighting

coins in our waist overalls.

SayDee could not contain her curiosity, "Why would grown bad men sew gold into their jeans?"

"Sewing small stacks separately into the pant legs would not allow the coins to hit against each other and give us away by the noise. It also allowed the horses to carry these small bags easier by tying the top of the jeans to the saddle and draping each leg on either side of the saddle."

Without a lookout, we bedded down with gladdened hearts and dreams of gold.

Chapter 9

It was now the Tuesday a week after the robbery; our provisions, which Collins procured in Ogallala, had run out. We had some coffee, and then we saddled up to continue our ride south. It was just before sundown when Collins told us to pitch camp on the other side of Sappa Creek. He and Berry were going to check out the homestead soddie just upstream. Maybe they could buy some food from the hoe man[32] who lived there. They found only a widowed lady and her children by the name of Anthony living there.

We picketed our horses and stretched ourselves out for a little rest before Collins and Berry returned. I and the rest had no more than stretched out on the ground when we heard Collins and Berry yelling as horses' hooves pounded the ground approaching our camp. I had just started to sit up when a horse and rider came through the thicket and d-m- near stomped me. I rolled over and quickly stood up. Collins and Berry were much closer now, and we understood them to be saying to "get that guy." We drew our pistols and began firing at the rider, who, at this point, was leaning over to the side of his horse's neck. Davis and Heffridge had gotten mounted and continued the pursuit with Collins and Berry. Davis and I holstered our revolvers and saddled up and joined in the hunt. The hunt didn't last long, and we quickly

[32] Term for a farmer

rode back to camp. It was then decided that this rider had been following us, and we needed to continue south with haste.

As we rode, Collins gave orders as to what pairs should ride together and the route each should take. Berry and I were paired. We initially struck out on the route Collins told to us go, but Berry said it wasn't good. He recalled his time with Bloody Bill Anderson and how they eluded the blue coats.

Berry lead the way continually in a southeasterly direction until we came to the South fork of the Solomon River. We rested our horses while keeping watch above the river. Within the hour, we mounted and crisscrossed the river several times along with riding in it. We rode through the night. Locating a heavy timbered, brushy area next to the river where it was joined by a creek coming from the southwest. We hid the horses and took turns sleeping. Berry told me we need to only travel at night and stay away from towns and homesteads whenever possible. My blood was pumping, and I didn't sleep much that first night. It was a damp, cold night; we awoke to fog settling along the river. Our horses needed rest desperately; they grazed freely along the creek where they were staked. Even though we hadn't eaten for two days, we didn't feel hungry.

Wednesday, September 26, 1877, sometime after dark, we again started in a southeasterly direction following the Solomon River's south fork. We rode all night, stopping at a small community which had a store. We waited in a distance until it opened in the morning. I was elected to go in and purchase provisions that we could eat immediately, being sure not to take any can or jar items. We then rode for another hour before dismounting in a thicket. We had carrots, potatoes, and dried biscuits that morning and were happy to have 'em. We again staked the horses close by and took turns as lookouts. This was our general routine for the next six days. Intentionally staying away from towns and people meant our eating was scarce.

When the river turned toward a southerly direction, Berry continued to ride east. The landscape was a series of shallow hills running north and south with shallow ravines. We saw fewer homesteads this portion of the trip. The days are short in October, and the nights longer, which allowed us to make a little more progress on our trip.

On Thursday, October 4, 1877, in the little hours of the night, we were approaching a sizeable town. We stopped in front of a small saloon on the outskirts of this town and entered the establishment, leaving our horses and gold outside. There were only a couple of drunks and the saloonkeeper. We had a beer, dried beef, and some stale crackers. We returned to the dark outside, riding away from the saloon but keeping an eye out to make sure nobody watched in what direction we rode. We camped beside a river adjacent to this town which was Marysville, Kansas. We were awakened by the sound of a train leaving town. Later in the day, we rode to the train depot and asked when the next train departed. The agent told us this was the end of the line for the St. Joseph and Western Railroad. The train leaves each morning at eight and arrives in St. Joseph, Missouri at eight at night. We purchased our tickets and rode off. Nothing seemed unusual around the depot or the town, so we rode out to discuss our plans for the next day. We decided to board our horses at the livery in the morning, deciding whether to leave our saddles, except the saddle bags, or else conceal the gold in a bed roll, which could be taken along. We camped at a different location along the river, taking turns as lookout once more.

On Friday the 5th, we were working at tightening our cinches when Berry walked over with a revolver in his hand.

"This is the pistol the express agent had. I already have two, and I think you may need another one. It has a short barrel, which makes it a nice belly gun or pocket gun. If you carry it in your coat, remember, if you attempt to pull it out in a rush, the hammer may hang up on the pocket. It's best to shoot through your coat. If anyone asks, we just finished driving a herd to the Dakotas and are returning home. You can make easy connections to Canada from Chicago. On the train, we will sit at opposite ends of the car facing each other, so we can protect each other's back. Once we get in the train car, we won't talk to one another. If you want to talk to me, take your hat off and run your hand over your head. I'll do the same if I need to talk with you. We then can meet on the back platform, but stagger getting out there; we don't want people thinking we are together. One of us always needs to stay awake as a look out. We should be ok on this leg to St. Joe."

It was just at sunrise when we mounted and rode into Marysville toward the livery stable. We kept quiet and only talked if necessary. I released my bed roll from my saddle and then retied the latigo tight on each end, making sure the coins were secure. We walked toward town and then turned back onto another street toward the train station.

We stayed in the alleys until we got closer to the train depot. Soon, we were standing on the platform waiting for the boarding call. My blood was pumping so fast I could have sworn a person could have seen my heart beat. Berry seemed cool and casual, as he looked around. Once we got on the train and it was moving, I felt some relief.

Chapter 10

The old man looked at SayDee, speaking in a quiet voice, "No questions, Miss SayDee?"

"I'm speechless; I don't know what to say. I'm having difficulty with understanding all you are saying. I mean, I understand what you're saying, I just can't grasp your thinking," SayDee replied with a confounding expression. She continued to say, "Please go on, there is got to be much more."

Sipping some water, the old man softly continued.

The train rolled on into the day, heading toward Missouri, and hopefully allowing us some breathing room from the railroad detectives, law officers, and anybody else looking for us.

I studied each person on the train to figure what they were. I didn't stare at them but looked their way from time to time. Finally, I sat back, and my mind drifted to that first time I had gotten on a train. It seemed funny now that a train had provided all the money I ever would need. As I was pondering what to do next, a thought came to me. I looked at Berry and eventually he looked back at me. I removed my hat and ran my fingers from the top to the back of my head. I returned my hat and, in a moment, I got up and walked to the back platform. I waited and waited, possibly for three minutes. Finally, Berry opened the door and stepped onto the platform. Berry asked, "What's up?"

"I'll be leaving you at St. Joe to head north to see

relatives in Minnesota and Michigan. I think I can make it along the Missouri river and not go by train. Thank you for guiding us this far. I can see why you were valuable to all of us now. I just wanted you to know." I turned and walked back into the car and returned to my seat. Five minutes later, Berry came back in and walked past me to his seat, not giving me a second glance.

Our arrival in St. Joseph brought little notice to the city. The train rolled into the station and took on other passengers while some of us got off. I asked a passerby which direction the river landing was from the station. I began walking slowly in that direction, always staying in the shadows. I soon found myself along the river's edge. I walked toward a building where the sign said "Rooms." I checked in using the name Charles Bright. I put the pistols on and alongside the bed, leaving the window partially opened for an easy escape if necessary. The soft bed swallowed me in sleep.

I awoke about mid-morning on October 6th; my heart was still pumping, and I wondered if it would ever be normal again. I had a dream that night, or maybe a premonition. In this dream, I was back on the train car with Berry. Everyone's face was frozen looking at me; those with the back of their heads to me must have been looking at Berry. Nobody moved. I just kept hearing a voice say, "Look and see!" Standing in front of the washstand, I looked at myself in the mirror, and the dream came flying back along with the words, "look and see." I stared at a reflection of a young man with long, greasy hair and a slight beard. In the dream, all the men were clean shaven with neatly combed hair and beards.

Their clothes were clean. They looked like town folks or hoe men going to town. Berry had long hair and beard both greasy and dirty. My clothes were trail worn and dusty. The light finally came to me. I needed to keep myself neat and clean so as not to draw attention to myself. I needed to blend in and look like everyone else, if I even hoped to get by. I remember what Berry said about staying away from towns, to talk very little when you meet someone, and leave very little trail. I decided right then to get cleaned up, buy new clothes, send a telegram, and get out of town as fast as possible.

I accomplished the first two things, getting cleaned up and new clothes. I looked like some drummer with a hard-boiled hat carrying his valise walking to his next sale. The telegram was the next item which needed to be completed before I left town. I thought it would be best if I myself didn't go to a telegraph office, so I found a young man and gave him $2, which was more than the telegraph cost, to go in my place. I had written a note previously, which I handed the young man. He read it and understood what I was requesting of him. The telegram stated: "Benjamin Marks, Dollar Store, Cheyenne, Wyoming. Dad, Need freight car on October 9, same place and route as before. Mark freight boxes as furniture. Will re-pay. Tad Pole, watchman."

I watched the young man go down the street and enter the Western Union Telegraph office. Afterward, I began walking toward the river. On one of the corners, a newspaper boy was heralding news as he stood selling his papers. "Two train robbers shot and killed." I paused just briefly and walked toward the news boy. My mind went back to the other five and wondered who was killed. I also recalled the oath which we all took. More than ever, I realized the robbery of the train was a very deadly matter. I purchased a paper, which I tucked under the arm carrying the valise. I brushed my empty hand across my coat pocket, making sure the short barrel pistol was there. Next, I moved my hand upward along my coat, feeling the pressure of my other revolver against my waist as it rested between my trousers and coat. I continued to walk to the river's edge.

There were different types of boats and barges tied up. One was securing the load of building materials previously loaded. I guessed they would be shoving off soon. I asked to speak to the captain. He peeked his head out from the pilot's cabin. I asked if he would take me to Omaha. He said he would for payment of $10 and if I stayed out of the way of his crew. I agreed and stepped onto the boat. He told me where I could sit on the back of the boat. I followed his commands. In a short time, the captain started the side paddle wheeler, and we began our trip up the Missouri River. I gave a slight sigh as the boat pulled away. I glanced back at the shore to see who, if anybody, might be watching. I spotted no one.

I began reading the article in the paper about the killing of the robbers. I tried not to show any reaction as I read. It explained how a detective from the railroad had followed the gang as they headed south. Each day he would find a messenger to ride to Ogallala to telegraph the names, whereabouts, and direction the gang was headed. He mentioned in his first telegram they would be crossing the Kansas Pacific line. So, troops and a sheriff were sent out west along the line. All the station agents along that line were alerted. On Wednesday of September 26, two riders came out of the fog riding played-out horses and leading a pack pony, stopping at Buffalo station. The article said if they had kept riding, everybody would have thought two cowboys were heading back to Texas. But they stopped for some provisions. The agent engaged them in conversation and followed them over to Thompson's store where they both went in for food. While paying for the provisions, the agent noticed an envelope sticking out of the man's pocket with the name Collins on it. The agent pretended that he had seen Collins before and asked if his name was Collins. The man answered he was Joel Collins. The two men went outside and remounted, continuing their travel south. The agent went over to the sheriff Beardsley of Hays City, who came out on a special train with the troopers to look for the robbers. The agent told him those two were gang members who robbed the train in Big Springs, Nebraska. One was named Collins and they were both riding pot hook branded horses.

The sheriff left with half dozen troopers. Upon catching up with them, Sheriff Beardsley confronted them and said they fit the description of the train robbers and he wanted to question them to see if they have any gold.

Collins said the sheriff was mistaken and the two began to ride back the few hundred yards to the station. Collins spoke softly to the other gentlemen and then attempted to draw his revolver, but the hammer got caught on a coat wrinkle. Sheriff Beardsley shot him in the heart. The other man also was drawing his revolver when a soldier fired a shot, which hit the man's heart. Both men fell from their horses, dead. The paper said the two dead men were Joel Collins and Sam Bass.

I folded the paper and placed it inside my valise. I sat staring out, thinking about what the article said. Heffridge was to ride with Collins, after all, he was his right-hand man and was dependable in a tight spot. Why and when did Bass and Heffridge change places. How did they know all the horses except mine were branded with a pot hook? That detective puzzled me most. Who in the h—l was he? When was he close enough to hear our plans and to describe each of us and know where we were headed? I thought back to when we camped those first nights. No look out was appointed because we all thought nobody suspected us. Fools! We were d-m-fools.

Chapter 11

"Why would Mr. Collins have a letter in his pocket? Was it important?" SayDee's curiosity forced her to ask.

"It was a letter from his lady friend. He had left the Black Hills with her on a stage to Sidney, and then he rode to meet us north of Ogallala. He sure pined for that woman. He would take that letter out almost every night and read it to himself."

"You knew both Collins and Bass?" SayDee questioned the old man.

"Yup, except the paper reported it wrong. I think it was reported that way to throw the rest of us off our guard. Sam was not killed at Buffalo Station. He was shot to rags in Round Rock, Texas. It was Bill Heffridge who was killed at Buffalo Station. He also went by the name of William Potts. He used that alias because he was from Pottsville, Pennsylvania." The old man looked more sullen than previously. "It was Bill Heffridge, but the authorities didn't know it immediately. They took his body to Ellis, Kansas, and there he lay in state so anyone passing by might recognize them. Well, it was his former wife who identified him. He's buried there in Ellis, Kansas, to this day."

"I'm curious, never being around a horse, what is a pot hook horse?" SayDee asked in puzzlement.

With a big smile, the old man responded, "It's the

brand on the horse. A pot hook is just a backward J, that was the brand on the horses Sam brought back that night."

"Thanks for enlightening a tender foot," SayDee replied, smiling genuinely. She started asking other questions before the old man could continue. "So, you have relatives in Minnesota and Michigan?"

"I lied! I'll continue now." Drinking another swallow of water, he went on.

From then on, I told myself to get a paper each day if possible and read up to see what is going on and if there were any new developments in this robbery I participated in. I also wanted to know who the h--l this detective was who trailed us.

It was too dark to re-read the article again to obtain additional information. The boat pushing the barge arrived north of the bridge, crossing the Missouri River between Iowa and Nebraska, sometime before dawn. Where the barge moored that morning, called Florence, was speckled with houses and soddies. I asked the captain if there was an eating place, and he pointed to the top of the hill. Stepping ashore, I headed straight up the hill, where a couple of business had set up their establishments. I located a store, but it wasn't opened. I found an open-faced lean-to at the back, and I made myself comfortable for a few hours of rest. At gray dawn, I continued on my way west, proceeding further away from the community. Once the town was out of sight, I headed south off the trail toward the direction of the railroad bridge. Upon finding a suitable woods and thicket, I sat down to rest. Taking my bed roll out of the valise, I spread it out and took off the new clothes. I would draw suspicion from others if I was wearing dirty stained clothes. I laid the clothes neatly on the ground where I had brushed away the leaves. I rolled myself up in the bed roll and fell asleep. My sleep was restless that night; the faces of the gang members kept popping into my head. The snapping of a twig brought me up out of my roll with both revolvers in my hands. I sat there and listened for the longest time. Finally, I saw a deer spring from its cover. The twig snapping reminded me of the night when we were counting the gold, and we all heard a twig snap. That must have been that d-mn detective, not a horse.

It was the 8th of October; I only needed to spend one more night before I could get into that train freight car. That would hide me for at least two whole days. I knew this was Sunday, and I would not find many places opened. More people would be at home or sitting around their home place. I dressed and continued to walk toward the train freight yards. I arrived at the outskirts of the yard just before dark. I got a good look at the lay of the yard. I stayed between a few trees and kept out of sight. I noticed the watchmen make their rounds, observing where they went and what they checked. At night, the light of their lanterns told me they made the same rounds checking the same places. I decided to stay in these trees, away from the yard and the watchmen. Again, I removed the store-bought clothes, and, this time, I put on my soiled waist overalls and dirty shirt for warmth; the nights were getting cooler. Then laying out my bed roll,

I slept on half of it while covering up with the other half. My revolvers were at the ready. I slept somewhat better.

I was trusting Mr. Marks got my letter and that he would send the freight cars and boxes of freight. I sure hoped everything would be there come the next day. I did not want to think what I would do if nothing were waiting for me.

The birds began singing at sunrise, which is what woke me up. I quickly took off my dirty old clothes and put the store-bought clothes back on. My plan was to walk around the freight yard, hoping to find a café where breakfast could be purchased. I would also ask them to pack a lunch for me, as I would be traveling.

I was in luck; I found a café which was crowded with rail yard workers. I entered and noticed a newspaper on the counter. I picked it up and headed for a table in the back. Once I placed my order, I kept my head down reading, or at least looking like I was reading the newspaper. The place emptied out except for a couple of folks. I relaxed some and finished my breakfast. They brought me a big lunch, and I thanked them. The paper I had picked up was the same paper I had read on the barge coming upriver, so I left it on the counter where I found it.

I knew each time I encountered people, I would run the risk of someone recognizing me. I was only counting on the fact that the robbery took place miles away from this yard.

Full of food, I checked myself over; I needed to

pass myself off as an associate of Mr. Marks. All the while, I was hoping that none of these railroad men knew much or anything about the robbery.

I entered the yard man's office, asking if the freight car for Mr. Benjamin Marks had arrived. The agent glanced up briefly, and then he began shuffling papers. "Yes," replied the agent.

"What about his freight order?" I inquired.

"It is expected to be here any minute now," replied the agent.

"Good," I responded. "Did he book a passage for his watchman, Mr. Pole?" I inquired. Once again, the agent rifled through his paper and then said, "Yes sir. Are you Mr. Pole?"

"At your service," I said.

The agent spoke as he got up from behind his desk. "Let's walk down and get your car open so the freight can be loaded directly into the car and not sit on the dock."

We walked toward a line of cars which sat idle in the yard. He slid open the door. "Here are your papers for the car; you will need to get the loading invoice from the folks delivering the freight."

"Pardon me sir, since I'll be riding inside this car, will the door be nailed?" I asked.

"Yes sir!" the agent replied, curtly, "we are now required to do that on all freight cars."

I said I was sorry to hear that. The agent asked, "Why?"

"I may be out of a job pretty soon," I replied.

He smiled and then walked back to the freight house. I climbed up into the car thinking, "I'm almost out of here." I examined the car from the inside. Jumping back off the car, I finished my inspection by walking around the car. The freight to be loaded was arriving in a couple of wagons just as I got back to the door opening.

I told the men I was Mr. Pole, the watchman for Mr. Marks and that I needed to see the invoice for this freight. One man handed me papers, which I glanced through. They began unloading the crates from the wagon and placing them in the box car. I noticed a hammer and crowbar in the wagon bed, which I quickly put into my valise. When the freight was loaded, I returned to the freight office and told the agent the car was ready to go. I would be riding in a Pullman car, not inside the freight car. He just nodded and continued to shuffle his papers. I stepped outside and walked back to the car. There, I climbed inside and closed the door. I began to pry off the lid of the long crate which supposedly held a hutch. Opening the crate, I found it contained a few long pieces of lumber and some hay as stuffing. I nailed one corner shut and then climbed into the crate. The lid pivoted on the nailed corner to allow me to bring the cover completely over the crate opening. I was then secure inside this crate without being seen by anyone. I just had to wait until the yard men came by and nailed the car closed. The wait wasn't long. Shortly,

I heard the large pin being nailed into the loop on the door clasp. The cars were jolted as each was attached to the engine. Slowly, the train pulled out of the yard. My breath came easier.

Chapter 12

SayDee looked at the old man curiously. "So you trusted a man you only met once, and this man followed your instructions in your telegram. Why would he do that?"

"I honestly don't know. But I had nobody I could turn to for help. I just felt I could trust him when I needed help. It turned out I could."

"So, is that the end of your story? Have you expelled all now?" SayDee inquired.

"I would like to tell you the rest, if you will listen?" the old man asked.

"Sure, you got me on the edge of this chair, but I'm not sure I can believe all of this," SayDee confessed.

The old man began again.

That trip gave me two peaceful nights of sleep and one very good lunch. I felt rested as the train pulled into the Union Station in Cheyenne, Wyoming, on the evening of October 12th. I had spent my waking hours figuring out a way I could nail the lid shut from the inside, so I could get out when it pleased me. Early in the morning on the next day, I heard them open the train car door. I listened very closely, trying to recognize the voice of Mr. Marks. The crate I was in was lifted onto a wagon and slowly driven out of the train yard. I listened mostly to the sounds, trying to get an idea where I might be going. There was nothing that gave me a clue.

Maybe it was too early, and the town had not awakened. I could hear men talking as they lifted the crates and brought them into a building. "Careful with that big one. Don't put anything on top of it," a voice instructed from a distance. The crate I was in was set down, and shortly thereafter, a door was closed and bolted. I waited awhile and then began prying open the crate. Once I was out, I replaced the lid and nailed it shut from the outside. I sat there in a dark warehouse, trying to figure out how I could reach those high windows. I gave up and figured when someone came, I would jump them and get away from this prison.

It was near evening when footsteps approached. The movement of the bolt signaled it was my time to hide.

The door opened. "Tad Pole, are you in here? I brought some food and drink. You must be hungry form that long trip."

I wanted to answer but wasn't sure who was talking; it might be a railroad man.

"This is Benjamin Marks. You sent me a telegram. I hope you got into the long crate I sent."

I still waited, and then, when I heard his steps turn, I spoke up. "Mr. Marks, I'm here. I do thank you for sending the crates and train car. What do I owe you? I said I will settle up when I see ya."

"Come on out, and we'll talk; there will be time for settling of accounts later." I came up to him and shook his hand.

"WAIT! Wait!" exclaimed SayDee. "That's all you said, and then you shook his hand. No explanation of why you requested his assistance. No explanation of why you're in this circumstance?"

The old man shrugged as he continued, "Didn't see a need to draw him into something that I did. Besides, I said I would pay for his expenses. I felt that was enough explanation, and I wasn't going to tell him my problem."

"The minds of men and how they think I'll never understand," SayDee expressed in exasperation.

"I stayed at his business establishment long enough to get myself cleaned up and clean my cowboy outfit. I gave him $250 for the freight car, and, if I still owed him money, I would return in a year or two and settle up then. My plan was to cowboy on some ranch in Wyoming or Montana. Once I got my gear together, I told Mr. Marks I would move on. I asked him for another favor. I asked if he had a safe and if he would hold a valuable for me."

"Did he ask what it was?" SayDee blurted out.

"No!" responded the old man as he continued his story.

He moved me to the warehouse where the furniture was unloaded. The warehouse was located just a few blocks from the Union Station. I found a ladder and was able to reach the high windows, from which I could observe the movements at the Union Station.

I spent time observing the time when trains arrived and departed. I also observed the people coming and going, especially how they dressed. The times of arrival and departures created a lot of activity in and around the station. It was at those times I planned to enter the station to find a train and destination going north.

Winter was pressing at the door, and I had nowhere to go. It was October 15th; I planned to find a store where I could by an overcoat like the men were now wearing. In the back of my mind, I knew I needed to get away from people.

I went out onto the main street where I saw an Apothecary store. I decided to ask them where an overcoat might be purchased. Walking in, I spotted a small stack of newspapers laying on the counter. I picked one up and asked the clerk what store sells overcoats while laying down a copy of the newspaper and a dollar. I was told of a store a block further up the street. Picking up my change, I left with the paper and headed in the direction the clerk suggested. Before the hour ended, I was wearing a new overcoat and carrying a bundle containing warm winter shirts, wool trousers, and two sets of long drawers.

Before returning to the warehouse, I headed for the livery stable two blocks away. I stayed a distance away from the livery, observing the activity and if anyone was around. There were two men in the yard feeding and cleaning the corrals. Having assured myself nobody else was around, I walked up to the livery. My intent was to purchase a horse, but upon my arrival at the livery stable, my mind was changed. Tacked to the doorway was a wanted poster for Tom Nixon. I quickly removed it from the door, stuffing it into my coat pocket next to the short barrel revolver. I turned around, walking away from the livery taking a roundabout route back to the warehouse, my momentary place of relief.

Chapter 13

Once inside the warehouse, I secured the door and took the wanted poster from the pocket of the overcoat. Sitting on one of the chairs from a crate, I began reading the poster.

"What did it say? Was there some reward for you?" SayDee asked, inquisitively.

"A one-thousand-dollar reward, plus 10 percent of all the money recovered," came a frank response from the old man, continuing his story.

It described me as five feet seven or eight inches tall with blue-grey eyes, light hair, and whiskers. The whiskers were described as a beard not heavy or long, a mustache older and longer than the beard. It continued that I had worked as a blacksmith in Black Hills, and that I had friends in Minnesota and Indiana.

I laid it in my lap and did some serious thinking. The description was accurate. How did they get that? The color of my eyes was correct. Surely, the detective following us didn't get that close to see the color of my eyes. The hair and beard part was easy. "Worked as blacksmith in Black Hills" made it come together. There at the top of the poster it said, "Tom Nixon wanted, alias Tom Barnes." Some detective talked to the owner at the livery stable where I worked as Tom Barnes. That person supplied all this information. I never really told anybody my age; that was a guess. I might have looked twenty-five years old, but I wasn't. The poster also said I had $10 thousand dollars in $20 gold pieces dated 1877, minted in San Francisco.

The most puzzling part of the poster was the phrase friends in Minnesota and Indiana. I never told that to anybody. I did tell Berry that I could use the river to see friends in Minnesota and Michigan. It was then I realized they must have caught Berry. I quickly reviewed the columns in the paper.

On the bottom portion of the front page was a headline stating that the third robber was shot and captured. I began reading intently how James Berry's arrival in Mexico, Missouri, on the 8th of October was noticed and the following day he deposited large sums of money in three different banks. He then went on a drinking spree, exposing large rolls of bills having large denominations. The local Sheriff, Glascock, suspected he might be one of the train robbers since Berry never had anywhere near this amount previously. Berry wore his gun outside his coat, which was against the law, but many thought that was because he had so much money. Nobody approached him to question him out of fear. They knew he rode with Bloody Bill Anderson and law officers kept their distance. He continued his braggadocio style all week. E. M. Morsman, Superintendent of the Union Pacific Railroad, encouraged Sheriff Glascock to arrest him. But, by the time that happened, Berry had left town and was now out of the jurisdiction of Sheriff Glascock.

The detective who originally tracked the outlaws, M. F. Leech, was already hiding outside of the Berry household in Callaway County waiting for his return. On the evening of October 13th, Sheriff Glascock was told Berry's neighbor, Boze Kazy, was in town to pick up a suit Berry had ordered. The Sheriff intercepted Mr. Kazy as he was leaving town. The sheriff and five posse members returned with Mr. Kazy to his residence. Half a mile from the Kazy house, the sheriff tied up Kazy and left him with one posse member as guard. The sheriff divided the remaining members up with two going to the south and the sheriff and the youngest member went to the north and west. Each member of the posse had double barrel shotguns with buckshot.

A horse neighed in the distance; the sheriff and the young posse member crept toward the sound. They hid in the thicket and waited. A horse snorted; this time the sheriff crawled fifty yards and could see the back end of the horse. He kept crawling and saw Berry unhitching the horse from a tree and was leading the horse directly toward the sheriff. The Sheriff Glascock raised up and hollered "halt." Berry turned and ran; Sheriff Glascock fired a blast over his head, but Berry continued to run. The sheriff fired the next barrel into the legs of Berry. This caused him to fall rolling down a slight hill. He was stopped by a small sapling, which prohibited him from removing his revolver from its holster; the sheriff removed it for him. Berry asked the sheriff to finish him off.

Berry was taken to The Ringo House, where he was being attended by a medical doctor.

When I had finished reading that story, I returned

to searching the rest of the paper for any additional story. Upon reaching the third page, I saw a headline: "Identity of Train Robber Known at Robbery."

This article told how a Mr. Riley, the person shot during the Union Pacific train robbery, had recognized Joel Collins the night of the robbery. It seems Collins's neckerchief slipped down when it was caught on part of the coupler. Mr. Riley had met Collins two weeks before when he was in Ogallala attempting to conduct business with Mr. Riley. This information was not released the next day because the express train took all the passengers from the robbery to Omaha to be questioned by railroad detectives. Upon Mr. Riley's return to Ogallala, he was informed that Collins had been in town the day after the robbery.

F. M. Leech, a store clerk at Ogallala, offered his services as a detective to the railroad. He rode to the robbery site and began tracking the robbers back towards Ogallala. He saw where they buried the gold and then dug it up again, leaving some of their neckerchief masks at this location. Joel Collins had purchased six of these neckerchiefs from him a few days before. He also recognized a boot print from a pair of boots he had sold Jim Berry. He remembered this because two other men, Collins and Heffridge, had to put all their money together to purchase the boots.

Mr. Leech, in a short period of time, caught up with the robbers and twice entered their camp at night. He listened to their plans and where they were going. He would then find a rider and send the message in code back to the agent at Ogallala who would relay it onto

Omaha. That is the reason why the Hays Sheriff and army troopers were at Buffalo Station when Collins and Heffridge came riding into Buffalo Station that foggy Wednesday morning on September 26th.

It was learned later that Sam Bass and Jack Davis dressed as farmers and drove a wagon south somewhere west of Buffalo Station a day after Collins and Heffridge were killed.

The article continued, "F. M. Leech is a hero and a manhunter who is continuing to track the outlaws to this present time."

Upon finishing the articles, I now knew the name of the detective who was following us was a store clerk from Ogallala named F. M. Leach. I also remembered back to what happened in the days prior to the robbery, especially when I was waiting for everybody at Ash Hollow. Now, all of this is starting to get pieced together. This is what the detectives are doing. I realized I needed to stay ahead of them and away from places where they think I might be going. Now, I knew the name of the detective who followed us and how they got onto us so fast.

"Miss SayDee, you have referred to me as a liar, and I admit I have lied my way because I didn't want anyone to know my past. Being a liar is what kept me ahead of the detectives," the old man told the eager nurse.

I only told Berry about relatives in Minnesota and Michigan. But the poster said relatives in Minnesota and Indiana. I surmised Berry told them only part of the truth to throw them off track. Just as the newspaper originally said, Collins and Bass were killed at Buffalo Station. The gang members all said where they were going and what their plans were except me. Yeah, I said I was from Canada and wanted to buy a ranch up there, which was partially true. I wanted a ranch up there, but I wasn't from there. So, the detectives have false leads based upon my lies. This leaves me with places I cannot go to and things I liked doing that I can't do any more. I need to change how I think and begin doing things I haven't done previously. I need to become a different person. Berry went to his old haunts and continued living a careless lifestyle. The same was true for Sam Bass and Jack Davis. They didn't change how they lived; they continued robbing and stealing. I was determined to remake myself, while, at the same time, stay informed on what this F. M. Leech was doing and where.

I spent the rest of that day and night reading and re-reading the paper, attempting to determine what all the detectives might already know.

The next morning, October 16th, I dressed in my cowboy outfit, leaving the drummer outfit on a chair. I located a café which was full of hungover freighters and cowboys. Taking a small table in the very back, I looked over the room hoping there wasn't anyone there who could recognize me. Finishing my breakfast, I walked to the Apothecary store, where I purchased the day's paper. Before returning to the warehouse, I stayed in the shadows of a nearby building, observing the activities around the warehouse. Nothing was out of the ordinary, so I returned and locked myself back inside.

I began searching the front page, and, there on the bottom right hand portion was a headline; "Third Robber Killed," the headline screamed out. I read the article, and a few more details were given out about James Berry. He had died from his wounds and was under morphine after he was questioned by Sheriff Glascock. Berry did say his associate was with him when he disembarked from the train at Mexico. His companion took the Chicago and Alton train north. The article also said Berry's mother died just two hours prior to his death.

"Now there is just you and another man alive. You told me Sam Bass was killed; if three of the gang has been shot to death, then only you and one other robber still remain alive," SayDee stated, straightforwardly.

The old man looked out into the distance, then answered, "At this time, one month after the robbery, three of us were still alive. Yes, Sam was shot in Texas, and Jack Davis was killed later in Oklahoma Indian territory. So, yes, I am the only one living."

SayDee's interest in the old man's story needed some clarification. "Sounds like you are the only one left. Berry didn't give you away on his death bed."

The old man paused a few seconds before responding, "No, he didn't give them everything about me. Just a few more places the detectives will have to chase me. I even read that a detective went to Clifton, Canada, because they located me there. The detective and whoever the man they were looking for shot it out at the Post Office. They both were killed, but no money was recovered."

Sadly, SayDee spoke, "This crime has cost a lot of people their lives. I'm sure that must bother you."

"Yeah, especially James Berry. Had it not been for his knowledge in eluding and hiding, I probably wouldn't have made it."

Changing topics, SayDee asked, "Did Mr. Marks let you stay at his warehouse?"

Pausing, the old man replied, "No! No, he did not."

Chapter 14

The door to the warehouse was being unlocked; I quickly hid behind the large crate I slept in. Both pistols were at the ready. The late morning light had not yet illuminated the inside completely. I waited behind the crate, expecting detectives to come rushing in. Instead, I heard a trunk being dragged across the floor and someone calling my name. The second time my name was mentioned, I stood up with pistols in my hands.

"Good morning to you, Tad," said Mr. Marks, continuing to drag a suitcase type trunk toward me.

"You and I need to have a talk. Come over here and sit down. I'm sure you have been reading the paper these past couple of days. I'm not an idiot, and I don't like to be used. I figured you are one of those train robbers. When your telegram arrived, I thought you were in need of help and wanted to get out West, as you first said. Then, you asked me to store in my safe your valise. The past couple of days, I was reading about the latest happenings pertaining to this train robbery."

"I'm a gambler… an honest gambler. I am not a thief or a robber. I cannot be part of or get mixed up in the pit you dug for yourself. I'm telling you to leave, and I am wishing you the best."

"I will help you store your belongings in a bank's safe, but not mine. I have put some items in this suitcase you may find helpful. I have made an appointment with Mr. Converse, the President of the First National Bank.

They have what is called safety boxes you can deposit valuables therein. I told him you asked me if I knew where you might store some valuables. You came to my establishment as a customer looking for some direction, since you are new to the area. Do not give him the impression you know me. I don't want the detectives coming around asking me questions."

I interrupted him, "But he may recognize me, there is a wanted poster out on me."

"I know, I have seen it also. That just confirmed to me that you are one of those train robbers. But I know a little about Mr. Converse; he has a roving eye. He doesn't come into my establishment, but he looks. So, I have arranged for Alice to assist you. You can identify her as a traveling associate. She will meet you at the bank entrance. Take this suitcase, your valise is inside, and deposit your valise. Bring the suitcase back outside with you. When the two of you leave the bank, a carriage will be waiting; Alice and the suitcase are the only things that will get into the carriage. You, my young friend, are on your own thereafter. Be in front of the First National Bank at three o'clock sharp! Don't be late! I don't believe we will see each other again; I do wish you safe travels, and your life will be difficult for some time. We make choices in life, but each choice brings certain consequences. Some we can handle and keep going, others may cause an early demise. Fair well, Tad."

He turned around and walked back outside, securing the door behind him. I sat there and felt quite glum. In a few minutes, I opened the suitcase. Inside was my valise, which I opened. The waist overalls were there still securing the gold coins, just as I had sewed them that night. I also found a wig, a pair of work shoes, long trail duster, a pair of glasses, an oversized Irishman's cap, and a bottle of hair dye.

I tried the long trail duster on; it covered most of my clothes and allowed me to hide my revolvers. I next put on the wig and glasses. I went to a mirror which was stored in the warehouse and looked at my reflection. The wig made it all look phony. I removed the wig, duster, and glasses, and put on the Irish cap. This gave me the appearance of a dude from back East, except for my footwear. I sat down and tried on the work shoes. The footwear gave the outfit the appearance of someone from the East. I had found my outfit for entering the bank.

I next looked at the bottle of hair dye, and read the directions. There wasn't enough time for me to apply it and clean myself up, so I decided to hold onto it; it may come in handy someday.

Once I deposited my valise and left the bank, I would return here and change clothes, taking only what I needed and nothing more.

I met Alice at three o'clock as planned. She was a real shiner. Never before had I seen such a woman. She wore some type of fur coat and her dark hair hung down in ringlets. We entered the bank and asked to see Mr. Converse. The two of us were ushered into his office, and the door was closed. Once inside the office, after introductions, Alice removed her coat. She had some sort of see-through gown, or, at least, it appeared that way. Besides, she was moving her body to attract Mr. Converse's attention.

I stated my desire to store my valuables in a safety box at the bank. Mr. Converse barely looked at me and just filled out the papers, then got up and opened his door, asking a teller to take me to the vault. I left while Alice and Mr. Converse stayed in his office. I was given a key to a box inside a safe which would hold my valise. The teller inserted his key, and then, with my key, I opened the box. The teller left, and I was alone to remove the valise from the suitcase. I returned to the office and bade my farewells to Mr. Converse; Alice did the same, but, again, he paid little attention to me. Alice walked out of the bank without wearing her coat and nobody notice my departure.

"That was how Mr. Marks said he would help you. Alice was a distraction. Or maybe an attraction, so you would not be so noticeable," SayDee stated, assuredly.

"Yeah, it sure worked, I don't think I was there more than ten minutes."

SayDee, looking puzzled, asked, "What name did you give when opening a safety box account?"

"Thad Pole is the name I signed the form with. I wasn't even sure I would be able to get back to recover this treasure. It would be safe from thieves, and I should be able to recover it sometime in the future."

I walked back to the warehouse using a different route and observed the warehouse from a distance before returning and locking myself inside.

I changed into my warmer clothes, leaving my drummer outfit on the crate. I laid all the clothes I would take onto my bedroll, along with the hair dye, then rolled it tight. I wore the duster, work shoes, and large cap. I was going to keep the glasses, but I heard that voice, "look and see." It was then I realized people with glasses stand out; they are not common. From now on I needed to be a common man. I left the warehouse and was at the livery stable by four o'clock. I purchased a horse and tack and was on the trail riding away from Cheyenne, Wyoming, on October 16, 1877.

Chapter 15

"Where did you go?" SayDee inquired.

"I rode toward Fort Laramie, thinking I could blend in with the Army or something. I used a little of that hair dye, dabbing in small amounts. I was afraid it might not look right and that would draw attention to me. Well, it turned out that was the thing to do. It darkened my hair only a little."

"When I got to the Fort, I looked up the sutler, and he told me the Army was looking for laborers to build the new Fort Custer up in Montana. He was going to load up supplies and head in that direction. I asked if he hired help. If I had a wagon, he would hire me to go along. I said I didn't have one at the time, but I was sure I could get one. I was able to buy a used wagon from the Army, and I was headed to Montana away from people and was employed. So began my career as a shotgun freighter[33]."

"It was interesting at Fort Custer; I was on a burial detail to assist in burying the soldiers who died with Custer in 1876."

"How long were you there?" SayDee asked.

"I stayed in Montana building other forts and came back to Cheyenne in 1880," the old man replied.

[33] A freighter with one wagon; it hauled specialty items including: eggs, flour, potatoes, whiskey, and sometimes cats.

"Weren't you afraid you might be recognized by Mr. Leech or some detective?" SayDee asked as she tightened the blankets around the old man.

"Mr. Leech kept on my trail, I guess, for a year but never seemed to get close. By now, I was the only one left. Besides, Mr. Leech began chasing other outlaws. When an outlaw by the name of Doc Middleton came on the scene, he seemed to take all of Mr. Leech's time."

SayDee interrupted, "How do you know this?"

"The Army officers at these forts wanted a good library, and they wanted it stocked with current newspapers. I found that out and made arrangements so I could have all the old newspapers. I was able to stay pretty current with all that was happening both in the frontier and back east."

"What about the railroad detectives?" she asked.

"Oh, there were so many more train robbers, and they, too, had their hands full chasing them all over the country. The Butch Cassidy Gang seemed to occupy most of their time. I more or less began to fade into the past. After 1878, I hardly ever saw a wanted poster for me. I continued to dye my hair until I started to lose it. The weather in Montana requires one to wear some head covering, so that kind of prevented most of my hair from being seen. I also stayed clean shaven, which was unusual. That did draw attention to myself, but it worked out."

Bringing the old man another cup of coffee, SayDee asked, "Did you ever see Mr. Marks again?"

"I returned to Cheyenne in 1880 and planned to remove my treasure from the safety box at the First National Bank to some bank closer to Montana. I went to the bank where I renewed my acquaintance with Mr. Converse and visited the vault. There, I removed fifty of the gold pieces. I found a nice box and wrapped the coins tightly inside the box. I gift wrapped the box, placing it inside another box, which I addressed to Mr. Marks at his Dollar Store. I did not personally see him, but later I read about his marriage to a lady named Mary[34] in 1882 and their move to Iowa. I did attend his funeral in Council Bluffs, Iowa, in 1919."

"After leaving Cheyenne in 1880, I returned to Montana and worked as a freighter hauling supplies and personnel for the building of Ft. Maginnis."

"I had made a pretty good living in Montana as a freighter, and I returned to Sioux City the same year Mr. Marks died. I worked as a night watchman for Bekins Moving and Storage; it was close to where I took a room."

"How did you get from Montana to Sioux City?" SayDee asked.

"I drove my wagon from Montana to North Dakota. By then, the wagon was pretty well worn out. I sold out in Bismarck, and I rode a horse to Yankton, South Dakota. From there, I took a train to Sioux City."

---

[34] Mary Marks died in Los Angeles, California, in 1928. Article by Preserve Council Bluffs, McGinn, Roenfeld April 29, 2020 .

"Did you bring your treasure with you?" SayDee inquired.

"No! The longer I stayed away from it, the better I seemed to get along. I had saved some money, and I was getting by as well as the next fella, especially with the night watchman job."

"The year before 1934, things began to change. Finally, in that year, Franklin D. Roosevelt abolished the gold standard. Nobody was allowed to possess gold."

"What did you do when that decree was passed?" SayDee asked, excitedly.

"I often wondered how I was going to convert all that gold coin into spendable dollars. Now, the government provided a means to accomplish such a task without questions."

"I took a bus to Cheyenne, Wyoming, and retrieved my valise with the gold inside. Before leaving the bank, I took out fifty $20 gold pieces. The very next bank I came across, I exchanged those fifty coins at the rate of $35 per ounce of gold. I was given $1750 for those fifty $20 coins. With that money, I got back on a bus and returned to Sioux City, Iowa. For the next few months, I would go to different banks in Nebraska, South Dakota, Iowa, and Missouri, exchanging the gold for greenbacks. One of the tellers explained to me that a $20 gold piece was called a banker's coin, meaning it was intended to simplify transfers of large sums between financial institutions and nations. As I thought about what he said, I reflected that back in 1877, the average pay for a month's wages was $20-$30. Now I understood why the double eagle coin attracted so much attention. Had it not been for the removal of the gold standard, I probably would have never been able to cash my treasure."

"What did you spend it on? Did you buy your ranch, or a freight business?" SayDee inquired.

The old man paused some before answering, "Naw. When I had the gold, I was afraid to spend it for fear somebody would find me out. Now that it was all folding money, I didn't really have a desire to purchase anything big. I was making a living and getting by. So, I just kept it, thought I would bury it. Didn't really have a plan."

Chapter 16

There was a brief silence before SayDee asked, "Are you done expelling?"

The old man looked directly into SayDee's eyes before he spoke. "Just a couple things left, and then I've spoken my piece. There was a gal that most of us heard of while we were in the Black Hills. I never saw her personally but, whenever her name came up, the boys spoke kind words about her. She seemed to cheer-up about everybody she spoke to. She just seemed to have that way about her."

"Do you remember her name?" SayDee asked, excitedly.

"I do. Everyone called her Joy, and that seems to be just what she brought to those she spoke with. So, I have a favor which I would like you to consider."

"What kind of favor?" replied SayDee, with her curiosity peaking.

"This Joy worked in a hog ranch also, yet kept this bubbly attitude, kind of like yours. So, I think you should change your name from Hawg to Joy. It really is a more fitting name for someone with the likes of you."

Before SayDee could respond, the old man kept on talking.

"Would you please get me another glass of water and bring back two other gals with you. I'll explain when you return."

SayDee got up and went into the cafeteria's kitchen and, within a minute, returned to the table where the old man sat slumped in his chair.

"Here are two ladies you requested and the glass of water," SayDee announced as she set the water down on the table next to an unfolded piece of paper.

"Ladies," began the old man, "I need you to witness this here Last Will and Testament I had drawn up. I have made arrangement in this will to pay you for your efforts. First, SayDee, spell your name for me and give me your address."

SayDee complied as she watched the old man print out what she said. Then, the next lady did the same. The third lady followed with her name and address. But their names were written on another page. SayDee paid little attention to where the old man was writing down the names.

"Thank you, ladies, now if you will kindly initial where I wrote your names."

The third lady initialed where her name was as did the second lady. Flipping a page as those two women left, the old man pointed to where SayDee should initial.

It was at that time that SayDee realized that the old man had put her in his will.

"What are you doing?" SayDee exclaimed.

"Doing what I see fit and proper in my sound mind as the paper says. Now, earlier this evening you said you could help me remove my load and help me cross over. I have done expelled what I needed to; now it's your turn. I will sit here and listen, but you may have to hurry, dawn is approaching."

With the old man's reminder, SayDee realized she would be relieved of her shift at seven o'clock this morning as she began to speak.

"You still have an amazing memory for a person of your years. Yes, I did say I would lighten your load, and I would help you to cross over."

"You have unburdened yourself of what you did in your life, yet you still are carrying the guilt of that crime and all the subsequent errors resulting from that crime. It seemed your ambition was not to be a thief but an expert liar. I can't say for certain, but I think you are still practicing that as you expelled your story. In my upbringing, I was told that the father of lies is the Devil[35], and, right now, I'm not sure if you aren't a member of his gang."

"Since the beginning of your expelling you have been looking back over your shoulder, always running away from someone or something. That must have been an awful tiring and difficult way to live."

The old man looked at SayDee with sad eyes when he spoke, "Yeah! I don't want to look back anymore; I want to have something to look forward to, but the distance is so short now."

[35] John 8: 44 NAS

SayDee adjusted the old man's chair away from the table, so she could place her chair directly in front of him. "Do you know who Jesus is? You said a pastor talked to your mother about Jesus, so you must know a little about him. At least you have heard of him."

"Well, he was a man and he was also God's son. God loves us so much he sent his only son to take our punishment for our transgressions and appease the wrath of God. God does not lie. God did this as a gift to those who would trust in Jesus. By trusting in what Jesus did, we have been justified, innocent of our transgressions. Jesus paid our penalty; he purchased us with his own blood."

"Once you have trusted in Jesus, you have become a new person. That's what you said you needed to become, a new person. Only you can put your trust in Jesus. The future of the people who trust in Jesus and what he did for them is eternal life. Everything we did wrong is corrected by Jesus. He took our punishment, so we can stand before God as an innocent heir to his family."

"Remember how you felt when you asked Mr. Marks to arrange for a freight car and those crates of furniture. You trusted he would come through for you. That is the same type of trust you need in Jesus. He has done this work of salvation for us, and, by trusting him, we are redeemed and no longer on the wanted list, so to speak. Jesus took the punishment we deserved, so we will not be punished when we trust in him. We can enjoy eternally living with God in heaven."

“Remember that you wanted to keep your drummer clothes clean, so people would see a salesman and not a thief. Well, God cannot look at us because our clothes are as filthy rags because of our sins. Jesus came and is offering us a new suit of clothes, spotless, and perfect. We just must put our trust in him; he is the only one who can save us as we can’t save ourselves.”

“You told me that you got along better the longer you stayed away from your treasure.”

“God is offering this treasure of life eternally with him through trusting in his son. But this treasure is one that you will want to stay close to. The closer you are to his son, the more peace you will find. The peace won’t be in this life, but in the life you will have in heaven.”

“Heaven is not going to be a place of momentary relief like the warehouse. It will be a place of joy, comfort, and happiness forever. You’ll be serving the King of Kings, doing something that you enjoy and doing it out of enjoyment for him. I believe your mother will also be there, if she knew Jesus like you told me.”

“Is this something you want to accept?” SayDee thoughtfully asked.

The old man’s response came quickly, “God doesn’t want someone cut from the cloth I came from.”

Smiling at the old man, SayDee continued, “Oh, you are so wrong, God loves you and is waiting for you to come home. God tells us stories of those who have done so many things wrong, and he has brought them into his heavenly home. There was a king who committed adultery and then killed the women's husband. There was one of Jesus's gang members who denied him saying he didn't know him when he was arrested, not just once, but denying Jesus three times. Jesus still loved him and forgave him of his wrongdoings. Then, there were the two thieves who were hanging on crosses either side of the cross Jesus was nailed to. One kept mocking him, and the other asked for forgiveness. The one who sought forgiveness Jesus promised him that he would be in heaven with him that same day. He confessed his wrongdoings and accepted that Jesus could save him. He didn't exactly know how, but he trusted that he could. That is kind of where you are. So, you can see there is a hope, but you are the only one who can speak to him. You are the one who needs to confess your transgressions and put your trust in Jesus. I can't do that for you. But I told you I would help you to have all your burdens lifted."

"Listen to Jesus inviting you to have eternal life with him when he said, 'Come to me all you who are weary and heavy-laden, and I will give you rest. Take my yoke upon you, and learn from Me, for I am gentle and humble in heart; and you shall find rest for your souls[36]'."

"Take some time to ask God's forgiveness and to place your trust in his son Jesus. Talk to him about anything else. He will listen."

[36] Matthew 28: 28, 29, 30. NAS

"I'll get you another water or coffee, so you will have some moments to yourself with your heavenly Father," SayDee ended.

The old man's eyes seemed to light up, "I listened to what you said, and I will pause a few moments with my creator. Can you see if I can get another one of those pills? I'm sure I will be ok just sitting here looking outside. I promise I'll be right here when you return."

SayDee looked intently at the old man a few seconds, "I'll see what I can do. Besides, my shift is almost over, I'll bring my replacement along too."

SayDee got up from the table and left the cafeteria. She paused briefly at the entrance to look back to make sure the old man was alright. He was just sitting there with his chin resting on his chest, writing on an envelope. She continued her way to the nursing station on the third floor.

Getting approval for another pain pill, she and her replacement headed downstairs to the cafeteria. Entering the cafeteria, they saw the old man sitting in the chair with his chin resting on his chest and his arms down along his side. Upon reaching his side, they noticed he wasn't breathing. After examining him, they both realized he was dead.

There on the table was an envelope which read in typewriter letters LAST WILL AND TESTAMENT. Below in writing, written with a shaking pen, were the words: "I yoked up with him. Thanks, SayDee. Tad Pole."

POSTSCRIPT

They laid him to rest in Potter's Field, a small marker bearing the name Tad Pole. It was ironic that he died on the day and month that he robbed the Union Pacific railroad train. SayDee was the sole beneficiary of the will. The two witnesses were to be paid $250 each by SayDee.

A week later, with the will in hand, SayDee took a streetcar to the rooming house at the corner of Third and Perry Streets. His room was the first one on the right from the front entrance. Unlocking the door, her attention was drawn to all the newspapers stacked around the bed and against the walls. There were two windows, one overlooking Perry Street and the other overlooking Third Street. She thought Tad was being careful, as he still watched his surroundings.

The closet contained three dingy white shirts, two stained blue trousers, and one clean and pressed watchman's uniform complete with a badge. A slight smile crossed SayDee's face, remembering Tad talking about a star packer.

The dark shadow inside the closet concealed momentarily the black leather valise resting on the closet shelf. Pulling it from the shelf, its weight surprised SayDee. Laying it on the bed, she opened it and peered inside. Two revolvers lay just below the opening. Without taking them out, she moved them slightly, which revealed a pair of jeans. She wanted to remove the contents but restrained herself. Closing the valise, she picked it up and left the rooming house. She walked directly into town to the First National Bank. There she arranged for a safe deposit box large enough to store the valise with its contents.

Returning to her apartment, she sat drinking coffee, remembering what the old man had told her. The end will bear out if it's a tale or if it's the truth. Without seeing everything which the valise held, she began to understand the burden this ill-gotten treasure placed on the old man. His partners in crime all were killed, and he lived in a self-imposed prison. He couldn't do or have what he desired. His freedom of movement was curtailed, and he was left with loneliness and isolation. He never had anyone to share anything with. No wonder he wanted to expel to somebody.

SayDee pondered what she should do. November brought her back to the bank, so she could visually inventory what the valise's contents were holding:

Two pistols, the bigger one in a holster.

One pair of jeans showing parallel stitches across each pant leg with depressions of holding circular objects.

Thirteen packets with various paper bank wrappers indicating each packet contained $1,000.

Seven $100 bills and nine $10 bills.

A wrinkled wanted poster for Tom Nixon.

Six $20 gold pieces minted in San Francisco bearing the date 1877 were taped to the bottom.

SayDee left the bank, returning one month later, with a look of determination. She removed the thirteen packets, which amounted to $13,000. Leaving the bank, she walked down the block to a stockbroker's office.

She purchased thirteen $1,000 bonds, each with a term of thirty years, issued by the Union Pacific Corporation, which was the parent company of the Union

Pacific Railroad. Each bond would pay two and seven eight's percent annual interest.

A week later, she took out the seven $100 bills and paid her nursing loan debt.

In 1945, she began researching records to determine what happened to Tad's mother and Boris. She couldn't obtain much of any information. But she did find a record of a white woman being buried in Potter's Field in 1872, who was bludgeoned to death. Her name was Hattie Polly Poleman.

SayDee continued to work as a nurse for twenty years. Each year, around the end of October, she gave a donation to various charities in Iowa, Nebraska, and South Dakota. It was at that time of year when the Union Pacific Corporation paid the interest on the bonds she invested.

She eventually changed her name to SayDee Joy Hawg. Thirty years after purchasing those bonds she recouped the $13,000 investment. This allowed her to establish and administer a scholarship fund for young girls or boys to begin training in a technical field. She called it the Poleman Fund. She kept the six $20 gold eagles as a memento of Tad and his story.

BIBLIOGRAPHY

Adams, Andy. *Log of a Cowboy*, Skyhorse, 2014

Bryant, Jerry l. and Barbara Fifer. *Deadwood's Al Swearingen: Manifest Evil in the Gen Theatre*, Far County Press, June 2018.

DeArment, Robert K. *Man-Hunters of the Old West*, University of Oklahoma Press, 2017.

"History of Audrain County, Missouri", St. Louis: Historical Company, 1884. https://audrain.mogenweb.org/1884toc.htm

LeFevers, Delana. "The Biggest Heist in Union Pacific Railroad History Took Place Right Here in Nebraska", *Nebraska Magazine*, June 13, 2020. https://www.onlyinyourstate.com/nebraska/big-springs-heist-ne/

McNair, Abbey R. *All About a Line: The Sidney-Black Hills Trail's Impact on Cultural Landscape of Western Nebraska and South Dakota*, 2005, University of Nebraska-Omaha, PhD Dissertation. *Digital Commons*, 578. https://digitalcommons.unomaha.edu/studentwork/578

"Trail of the Train Robbers Begins", *New York Times Newspaper*, February 21, 1895.

Potter, James E. "'A Peculiar Set of Men': Nebraska Cowboys of the Open Range", *Nebraska History*, vol. 94, 2013, pp. 124-145. https://history.nebraska.gov/sites/history.nebraska.gov/files/doc/publications/NH2013Cowboys.pdf

Sorenson, Al. *Sam Bass Hands up! The History of a Crime*, Barkalow Brothers, 1877.

“The Leader Identified Inspite of His Mask”, “He Identified Collins”, *St. Louis Globe Democrat*, September 29, 1877

ABOUT THE AUTHOR

Warren Dunlap has been intrigued by the West and its history since he began wearing little britches. He was born with a vivid imagination and wanderlust to see the West. His first venture to head west was in "47", but his trip was interrupted when he was picked up and brought to the local jail.

Eventually, his dream did become reality. He ended up working for major corporations which sent him all over the West and various parts of the East doing research.

For most of fifty years he has worked, talked and listened to the tales of cowboys, ranchers and farmers. From his personal experiences and conversations, Warren Dunlap brings reality and authenticity to his stories.

Made in the USA
Monee, IL
04 November 2021

81085206R00075